T5-CCJ-434

"I'd already left town before you could possibly have known you were pregnant,"

Nick said, holding a piece of paper.

Chessa recognized the copy of her son's birth certificate. The cetificate with Nick's name on it. "I'd like you to leave now."

A peculiar sadness shadowed his gaze. "You know I can't do that." He stepped back, regarding her with unnerving intensity. "Chessa, you have every right to be hurt. But I want you to know that what we had together was very special."

All she could do was stare at him in utter awe. How gallant of him, she thought, to fake memories that didn't exist, about a relationship that never happened. Until five minutes ago, Chessa Margolis and Nick Purcell had never even met.

* * *

FOR THE CHILDREN

I Now Pronounce You Mom & Dad (SE #1261)
A Dad of His Own (SR #1392)
The Fatherhood Factor (SE #1276)

Dear Reader,

September's stellar selections beautifully exemplify Silhouette Romance's commitment to publish strong, emotional love stories that touch every woman's heart. In *The Baby Bond,* Lilian Darcy pens the poignant tale of a surrogate mom who discovers the father knew nothing of his impending daddyhood! His demand: a marriage of convenience to protect their BUNDLES OF JOY....

Carol Grace pairs a sheik with his plain-Jane secretary in a marriage meant to satisfy family requirements. But the oil tycoon's shocked to learn that being *Married to the Sheik* is his VIRGIN BRIDE's secret desire.... FOR THE CHILDREN, Diana Whitney's miniseries that launched in Special Edition in August 1999—and returns to that series in October 1999—crosses into Silhouette Romance with *A Dad of His Own,* the touching story of a man, mistaken for a boy's father, who ultimately realizes that mother and child are exactly what he needs.

Laura Anthony explores the lighter side of love in *The Twenty-Four-Hour Groom,* in which a pretend marriage between a lawman and his neighbor kindles some very real feelings. WITH THESE RINGS, Patricia Thayer's Special Edition/Romance cross-line miniseries, moves into Romance with *Her Surprise Family,* with a woman who longs for a husband and home and unexpectedly finds both. And in *A Man Worth Marrying,* beloved author Phyllis Halldorson shows the touching romance between a virginal schoolteacher and a much older single dad.

Treasure this month's offerings—and keep coming back to Romance for more compelling love stories!

Enjoy,

Mary-Theresa Hussey

Mary-Theresa Hussey
Senior Editor

Please address questions and book requests to:
Silhouette Reader Service
U.S.: 3010 Walden Ave., P.O. Box 1325, Buffalo, NY 14269
Canadian: P.O. Box 609, Fort Erie, Ont. L2A 5X3

A DAD OF
HIS OWN
Diana Whitney

ROMANCE™

Published by Silhouette Books

America's Publisher of Contemporary Romance

If you purchased this book without a cover you should be aware
that this book is stolen property. It was reported as "unsold and
destroyed" to the publisher, and neither the author nor the
publisher has received any payment for this "stripped book."

To Heather MacDonald,
who has been a joy, a friend and an inspiration.
Thanks, Heather, for being the beautiful person
that you are.

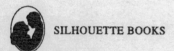 SILHOUETTE BOOKS

ISBN 0-373-19392-0

A DAD OF HIS OWN

Copyright © 1999 by Diana Hinz

All rights reserved. Except for use in any review, the reproduction
or utilization of this work in whole or in part in any form by any
electronic, mechanical or other means, now known or hereafter
invented, including xerography, photocopying and recording, or in
any information storage or retrieval system, is forbidden without
the written permission of the editorial office, Silhouette Books,
300 East 42nd Street, New York, NY 10017 U.S.A.

All characters in this book have no existence outside the imagination of
the author and have no relation whatsoever to anyone bearing the same
name or names. They are not even distantly inspired by any individual
known or unknown to the author, and all incidents are pure invention.

This edition published by arrangement with Harlequin Books S.A.

® and TM are trademarks of Harlequin Books S.A., used under license.
Trademarks indicated with ® are registered in the United States Patent
and Trademark Office, the Canadian Trade Marks Office and in other
countries.

Visit us at www.romance.net

Printed in U.S.A.

Books by Diana Whitney

Silhouette Romance

O'Brian's Daughter #673
A Liberated Man #703
Scout's Honor #745
The Last Bachelor #874
One Man's Vow #940
One Man's Promise #1307
**A Dad of His Own #1392

Silhouette Intimate Moments

Still Married #491
Midnight Stranger #530
Scarlet Whispers #603

Silhouette Shadows

The Raven Master #31

*The Blackthorn Brotherhood
†Parenthood
‡Stork Express
**For the Children

Silhouette Special Edition

Cast a Tall Shadow #508
Yesterday's Child #559
One Lost Winter #644
Child of the Storm #702
The Secret #874
*The Adventurer #934
*The Avenger #984
*The Reformer #1019
†Daddy of the House #1052
†Barefoot Bride #1073
†A Hero's Child #1090
‡Baby on His Doorstep #1165
‡Baby in His Cradle #1176
**I Now Pronounce You Mom & Dad

Silhouette Books

36 Hours
Ooh Baby, Baby

DIANA WHITNEY

is a three-time Romance Writers of America RITA finalist, *Romantic Times Magazine* Reviewers' choice nominee and finalist for Colorado Romance Writer's Award of Excellence. Diana has conducted writing workshops, and has published several articles on the craft of fiction. She is a member of the Authors Guild, Novelists, Inc., Published Authors Network and Romance Writers of America. She and her husband live in rural Northern California, with a beloved menagerie of furred creatures, domestic and wild. You can write to her c/o Silhouette Books, 300 East 42nd Street, 6th Floor, New York, NY 10017.

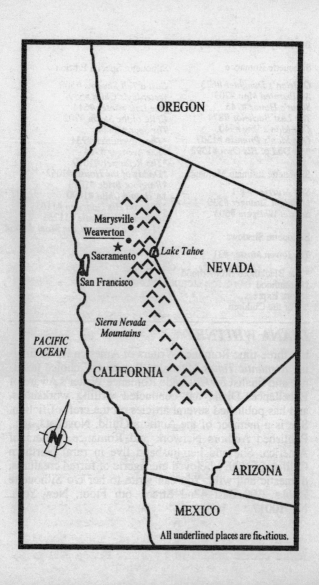

OREGON

^^^
Marysville •
Weaverton •
★ Sacramento
San Francisco

Lake Tahoe

NEVADA

Sierra Nevada
Mountains

PACIFIC
OCEAN

CALIFORNIA

ARIZONA

MEXICO

All underlined places are fictitious.

N

Chapter One

"Chocolate chip. Cool." Bobby Margolis plucked a cookie from the heaped platter and took a healthy bite. "Umm...good." Between chews he remembered his manners. Wiping a moist crumb from his chin, he managed a hasty swallow, a sheepish grin. "Thanks."

"'Tis welcome you are, lad." A wrinkly woman with hair like cotton balls set the platter on a doily-draped table next to his glass of milk. "Help yourself now. A growing boy needs nourishment."

"Okay." He took another cookie, slyly palmed a third for later. Mom always said it was rude to be greedy, but he'd sneaked away from the class outing before lunch, and his stomach was rumbling like an old school bus on a bumpy road.

Humming softly, the nice lady with the pretty smile busied herself laying fancy napkins beside the platter of warm treats, pretending not to notice the extra cookie hidden in his hand. Bobby was pretty sure she'd seen him take it, though, because her eyes got all twinkly, and her mouth kind of twitched the way Mom's did when she was trying not to laugh.

A sweet fragrance wafted around him as the lady moved, a scent that reminded him of the funny heart-shaped packets his mother laid in closets and drawers. Lavender, she called it, and said it made things smell good. Only Bobby didn't want his underwear reeking like girl stuff, so Mom had promised to keep all her flowery junk out of his bedroom. Mom always kept her promises. Well, not always. There was one promise she hadn't kept.

That's why Bobby was here.

He swallowed, squirmed, twitched his sneakered feet, which dangled several inches above the gleaming hardwood floor. "So when do I get to meet the lawyer?"

"You already have." With an amused tilt of her head, the lady's face spread into a wreath of wrinkles that made her look about a million years old. "Clementine Allister St. Ives at your service, young man." She extended a leathery hand with swollen knuckles that were all red and lumpy.

Arthritis, Bobby thought, on account of his great-great-aunt Winthrop, who was his gramma's mother's sister, had arthritis, too. It made her hands all bumpy and swollen, and she said it hurt, so he was careful not to squeeze Clementine's hand when he shook it. "You don't look like a lawyer." His gaze wandered across to a wall papered with old-fashioned flowers and studded with framed certificates. There were school names he didn't recognize—Harvard, Stamford, Berkeley—and all kinds of peculiar terms that he'd never seen before. He knew what attorney-at-law meant, but he didn't know what professor of genealogy was, and some of the other terms confused him as well. "What's a fid?"

Clementine followed his gaze, smiling. "That's a Ph.D. certificate, lad, a doctorate degree in psychology."

Bobby sat up straighter. "You're a doctor, too?"

"Not in the medical sense." She settled into a big wooden rocking chair, flinching slightly. "I counsel families now and again."

"Counsel?" The word evoked an unpleasant image of his elementary school vice principal lecturing kids about chewing gum and homework. "I don't like counselors. They're always bawling people out."

"Bawling people out, are they?" Clementine regarded him kindly. "Well, lad, as my sainted da used to say, if God didn't want folks to listen more often than talk, He wouldn't have given them two ears and only one mouth."

A tubby gray cat peeked out from behind a frilly lace curtain, then hopped onto the woman's lap. She idly stroked the animal, which curled comfortably under her squishy bosom and purred so loud Bobby could hear it all the way across the room. The animal diverted Clementine's attention long enough for him to surreptitiously snag another cookie.

"I got a cat," he announced between bites. "His name is Mugsy. I want a dog, too, but Mom says a dog would be too lonesome, on account of she's at work all day and I'm at school."

"Are you now?" Reaching for a manila file on the desk beside the rocker, she retrieved her dangling glasses, slipped them efficiently into place. "And what grade would you be in?"

"Fourth." Bobby figured she should know that, because he'd filled out a form for the pretty lady who worked in the front office. Deirdre, her name was. She had really nice eyes and a laugh that made him go all wiggly inside. She'd spent a lot of time with him, asking his address and stuff. She'd wanted to know what his birthday was, and that's when he'd given her the birth certificate that he'd sneaked out of the metal box Mom kept in the back of her closet. Deirdre had made a copy of it.

Squinting at a document inside the file, Clementine ignored the cat batting at the pearl-studded loop dangling from her funny-looking spectacles. "So you'd be nine years old, would you?"

"Nine and a half." He swallowed, reached for the glass of milk and drained half of it in a single swallow. "I'll be ten in March." He started to wipe his mouth with his sleeve, then noticed the stack of linen napkins Clementine had laid by the cookie platter and used one of them instead. "Mom says I'm smart for my age."

"That you are, laddie, that you are." Wise blue eyes twinkled over lenses that looked like they'd been chopped in half. "You must be a crafty young man to have found your way into San Francisco all by yourself."

Bobby shrugged. "It wasn't no big deal. My teacher got a big bus to take the whole class to the museum today, so when the rest of the kids went inside, I ran around the corner and looked for a cab."

"Ah, how clever. Don't you think your teacher

might be a wee bit perturbed when she notices you're gone?''

"Nah. If she asks where I am, my best friend, Danny, is gonna tell her I'm in the bathroom.'' Bobby glanced at an ornately carved wall clock positioned between a pair of intricate tapestries. ''Only I've gotta be back by two o'clock, 'cause that's when the school bus is gonna be back to take everyone home.''

"And home is—'' she adjusted her glasses, peering down at the file ''—in Marysville? That's quite a distance. How is it you decided to visit me instead of enjoying the museum with your class?''

Bobby sucked in a breath. His hands were sweaty and kind of cold, so he wiped his palms on his jeans. ''A long time ago you helped my friend Danny get adopted. He told me I should call you, on account of you're real good at finding parents for people.''

"I see.'' Clementine studied the open file. She looked sad, so Bobby figured she was looking at his birth certificate. His whole name was there, Robert James Margolis. So was his mom's, along with the name of a man he'd never known.

"Can you find my dad?'' Bobby blurted.

"Ah, so it's your father you're seeking, is it?''

Without warning, Bobby's throat went dry, and his eyes went wet. He laid the half-eaten cookie aside, took another healthy swallow of milk. His heart was beating really fast, and his hands were still cold.

Closing the file, Clementine rocked quietly for a moment, stroking the sleeping cat in her lap. ''Your mum doesn't know you're here, does she, child?''

Bobby sniffed, shook his head. ''She doesn't like to talk about my daddy. I think she figures it'll make me sad." Actually, Bobby had only asked her once, when he'd been just a little kid. Her eyes had gotten all red and watery. She'd promised they'd talk about it when he was older. Bobby was older now. He was almost grown up. But his mom had broken her promise.

Squaring his shoulders, he hiked his chin, willed his lip to stop quivering. "I brought money." Digging into his pocket, he retrieved a crumpled wad of bills, $18.65 that represented his life savings. He plunked it all beside the cookie platter, then remembered he'd need cab fare, and stuffed five dollars back into his pocket.

Noting a peculiar expression on Clementine's wrinkled face, he quickly added, "I got more." Squirming in the chair, he pulled the boom box reverently into his lap. It had been a Christmas gift from his mother, and was his most treasured possession. "This is worth a whole bunch of money, maybe even fifty dollars. It has real good sound. You can make it so loud that the speakers puff out. It's got bass and treble adjustments—" he demonstrated with a flick of the slide bar "—and it plays tapes and CDs and all the cool radio stations. It's really neat."

Clementine's smile was kind of sad. "Is it now?"

"Want me to turn it on for you?"

"That won't be necessary. 'Tis a fine instrument, to be sure."

"Oh." Swallowing a stab of disappointment at not being able to play his beloved music one last time, he reached inside his shirt, pulled out a wrinkled envelope with the name of the man he'd yearned for all his life. He touched the smeared ink with his fingertip, then passed the envelope to Clementine. "It's a letter to my dad, for when you find him."

She took it gently, cradled it in those gnarled hands as if it were as fragile as a butterfly. "Tell me why you're wanting to locate him after all these years."

The request surprised him, made him think for a moment. "'Cause there's gonna be a father-son picnic next month, and I don't wanna get stuck with dorky old Mr. Brisbane again."

"Mr. Brisbane?"

"Yeah. He's the school janitor, and he always partners up with kids who don't have dads so they don't feel, you know, left out and stuff."

"That's very nice of him."

Bobby shrugged. "Yeah, I guess, only I'm sick of borrowing dads all the time. I want my own dad."

"Of course you do," Clementine murmured. "Every boy deserves a father of his very own."

Hardly daring to breathe, Bobby leaped to his feet, clutching the boom box to his chest. "So you'll do it, you'll find him for me?"

"I'll do my best, lad."

A tremor of excitement shook him to his sneakers. He heaved a sigh of relief, and would have laid the boom box on Clementine's desk had she not extended a hand to stop him.

"You keep it safe for me, child, until I find just the perfect place for it."

He swallowed hard. "You mean it?"

"I do indeed. Deirdre?" In less than a heartbeat the pretty, dark-haired woman stepped into the room. "Will you please call a cab for young Mr. Margolis? He has a bus to catch."

Deirdre flashed Bobby the brightest smile he'd ever seen in his whole life. "Of course."

At the doorway, Bobby hesitated, glanced over his shoulder. "Danny was right. You're a real nice lady."

Clementine's chuckle startled the snoozing cat. "Thank you, lad."

His gaze flickered to the small wad of bills and scattering of coins on the corner of her desk. Chewing his lip, he motioned to Deirdre, who bent down so he could whisper in her ear. "Do you think that's enough money?"

"More than enough," Deirdre whispered back. "Clementine doesn't care about the money."

"Then why does she do stuff?"

"For the children, of course. It's always for the children."

The house was larger than he'd expected, old and quaint, with fading gray clapboards and a covered porch hung with a riot of blooming flowers. A pair of peaked-roof dormers protruded from the second story like startled eyes keeping watch on the neighborhood. The lawn was sparse, closely clipped but barren in spots, as if well used by the same children who played there now. Happy laughter echoed in the dry autumn air, a universal symbol of boyish joy.

A fat gray cat sprawled on the porch rail, tail twitching in time to the music blasting from one of those massive portable stereo units with speakers powerful enough to blast paint off a wall. It blared with the pulsing discordance popular nowadays, although the undulating rhythm made his teeth ache and raised the fine hairs along his nape. Aggravating

adults was the purpose of youthful music. In that
context, the chaotic sounds emanating from the shiny
black boom box had done its job.

The entire image was enthralling, the scampering
children, the biting noise punctuated by thrilled
laughter, hoots of joy. Memories in the making, he
thought, sweet images of childhood that would some-
day be cherished beyond measure. Childhood was
such a fleeting thing. His own had ended all too soon.

From his vantage point across the street, he gazed
out his car window at the youngsters playing soccer
on the scuffed lawn. A gregarious blonde was the
leader, a shouting, whirling, whistling bundle of
knobby-kneed energy shrieking orders like a five-star
general, orders that his teammates cheerfully ignored.
A sweating, heavyset child puffed around the make-
shift field as if every step was an effort. Others encouraged him, included him, although it was painfully apparent that the chubby child's soccer skills
were far below those of his friends.

Joining the game was a lanky youth with hair
shorn over the ears to leave a peculiar hank at the
crown pulled into a ponytail, and a youngster wearing a ripped football jersey who seemed to be the
clown of the group. He pranced, danced, cheered,
jeered and wiggled his bony butt at the slightest
provocation, much to the delight of his giggling com-
rades.

There was also a boy slightly smaller than the others, quieter, wearing a white T-shirt so huge it hung
nearly to his denim-clad knees. Tufts of straight
brown hair poked out from under a blue baseball cap
worn backward so the bill covered his nape, but exposed large, anxious eyes.

It was this boy who tossed a chummy arm around the heavyset child's shoulders when a kick-pass was missed. The smaller boy said something with a grin and a shrug that made the chubby youngster smile. He liked that.

In fact, he liked everything he saw. The hoots and hollers of kids at play, the sweaty little faces and the whirling energy of youthful exuberance on a clear Sunday afternoon. Even from a distance he could see that the boys were very different from each other, every bit as unique in style and personality even at this tender age as the adult men they would become. Each of them appeared happy, well cared for and loved. Each undoubtedly possessed special talents, specific gifts. Children at play, laughing, eager, filled with joy. A lump lodged in his throat as he watched, awestruck.

He wondered which one was his son.

"Bobby, lunchtime!"

"Aw, Mom, five more minutes, please?"

Stifling a smile, Chessa Margolis forced a parental firmness that had never come easily. Her son was the light of her life. She adored him beyond measure, and was loath to deny him anything, preferring to wheedle his acquiescence rather than insist upon it. "It's up to you, sweetheart, but the pizza will be cold by then."

"Pizza?" Bobby straightened, eyes huge, shoulders quivering. Rotating the black-and-white soccer ball in hands that seemed too small for the task, he angled an apologetic glance to his disappointed teammates. "Gotta go." He flipped the ball to his best friend, Danny, a skinny blond dynamo who lived two houses away. "Later, dudes."

Ignoring grumbles from his buddies, Bobby snatched up his beloved boom box, hit the porch running, dashed through the screen door his mother held open for him and skidded into the kitchen, sniffing the air like a hungry hound dog.

"Wash your hands." Chessa waited for Mugsy's unhurried entrance before releasing the screen door, which squeaked shut with a hollow shudder. "And take off that filthy hat before you eat." A peek into the kitchen confirmed that the grungy blue baseball cap had been hooked on a peg by the back door while Bobby scrubbed up in the kitchen sink beside a large bowl of whole peeled apples waiting to be sculptured.

Wiping clean hands on his dirty T-shirt, Bobby spun from the sink, bounced into the nearest chair and helped himself to a slice of the freshly baked pizza. He bit into it without a trace of fear, as if a blistered mouth was small inconvenience compared to the joy of devouring his favorite food.

Chessa turned off the blaring radio on her way to the sink, eliciting a muffled protest from her chewing son. "You know the rules. No television or music during meals."

Having polished off one slice of pizza, Bobby reached for another. "Danny's got a new pair of sneakers," he announced between chews. "They're really cool. You can pump them full of air and stuff."

"That's nice." At the sink, Chessa completed the apple processing with a diluted lemon juice bath, then set them into a colander to drain. Later that afternoon she'd carefully carve them, dry them and use the unique results to create country craft dolls that provided a tidy second income for Bobby's college fund.

"I wish I had a pair."

"A pair of what?"

"Air pumps, like Danny's."

"Oh. Do you have enough money saved up?" When he didn't reply, she glanced over her shoulder. He shook his head, avoiding her gaze. "How much more do you need?"

A limp shrug. "A lot."

"There are some extra chores around here I could use some help with." She set the draining apples aside and wiped her hands on a tea towel. "We'll sit down and count out exactly how much money you have, then we'll calculate how much more you need and—"

"Never mind." Pushing away his half-empty plate, Bobby leaped up from the table with startling speed and an expression that could only be described as apprehensive. "I don't want to count money and stuff."

"Managing finances for things you want is important, sweetie. You know that. We do it all the time. That's how you saved up for that remote-control car you love so much."

Eyes darting like a cornered cat, Bobby snatched up his radio, sidestepped toward the door. "Can I go outside now?"

"You haven't finished your lunch."

"I'm not very hungry."

"Not hungry for pizza?" She frowned, concerned

by the peculiar flush staining his cheeks. "Aren't you feeling well?"

"I'm okay, I just wanna go out—" A knock at the door spun him around, flooding his tense features with obvious relief. "That's Danny. Can I go, Mom?"

Heaving a sigh, she nodded, and watched her son bolt from the room. Bobby had been acting strangely for the past week. He'd been elusive, jumpy, even more anxious than usual. Just as disturbing was his refusal to acknowledge anything was wrong, let alone agree to discuss it.

Chessa knew her son, understood every nuance of expression, every subtle tilt of body language. He was hiding something, something that both worried and excited him, something that, for the first time in his young life, he'd chosen not to share with the mother who adored him.

Lost in thought, she retrieved a paring knife and was absently eyeing the peeled apple in her palm when a peculiar sound caught her attention.

She returned the apple to the colander, laid down the paring knife and listened. It was a man's voice, not a boy's. A man speaking quietly, gently, in a tone too soft for words to be deciphered. Bobby's response was choked, broken, inaudible.

Alarmed, Chessa rushed to the living room and nearly fainted. There he was, a specter from the past with the power to destroy everything she held dear.

From the doorway the man gazed over Bobby's head, expectantly at first, then his eyes slowly clouded with confusion. "It's been—" he paused, swallowed, studied her for a moment longer "—a long time."

Her mouth went dry. She steadied herself on the doorjamb. The room continued to spin. It was her worst nightmare.

This time it was real.

She was beyond beautiful. The woman staring at him as if seeing a ghost affected him like a punch in the gut. A twist of sable hair above a fragile, heart-shaped face with huge, liquid eyes so blue they took his breath away. It was a remarkable face, exquisite in its perfection even as its color dissipated to a sickly pallor. She clutched the doorjamb with a white-knuckled grip.

"Yes." A whisper more than a word. "A long time."

He wanted to sweep her into his arms. He wanted to beg her forgiveness for having abandoned her so very long ago. He wanted to heap blessings and gratitude upon her for having gifted him with such a precious son. Most of all he wanted to know why he couldn't remember ever having laid eyes on her.

This was a woman no sane man could forget.

Then again, Nick Purcell's youth had been anything but sane. Town bad boy, blamed for everything and responsible for much, he'd been an angry adolescent who'd risen above poverty and abuse by having removed most of it from his mind. He could barely remember those years, didn't want to remember them. That was his cross to bear, not this lovely woman's. Clearly he'd hurt her enough. Nick would rather gnaw off his own arm than cause her more pain by confessing his own failure of recall.

"It's wonderful to see you," he told her, and meant it.

She swayed slightly, those gorgeous eyes so wide the China-blue pupils were completely surrounded by white. Lush lips quivered, moved slightly.

A sob, a sniff, a small hand clutched his sleeve. "I knew you'd come, I knew it."

Dragging his gaze from the trembling woman, Nick knelt before the child whose eyes, as blue as his mother's, gleamed with moisture and excitement. Words choked in Nick's throat, caught behind a lump of emotion. Gazing into the face of his child was like a religious experience. His heart felt swollen, raw. His son, his flesh and blood. It was the proudest moment of his life. And the most poignant.

Bobby's chin quivered. "Are you really my dad?"

In the breast pocket of his suit coat, a folded birth certificate forwarded from the St. Ives Law Firm burned over his heart. "Yes, Bobby, I'm really your dad."

"Don't go away again." A tear slid quietly down his small cheek. "Please don't go away." With that, the child threw himself into Nick's arms, sobbing.

Nick hugged him fiercely. "I won't," he whispered, barely about to choke out the words. "You're my son, and I'll never leave you. Never."

The woman issued a strangled gasp. Nick barely heard it.

This wasn't happening.

Icy fingers of fear closed around Chessa's throat. Terror choked her dry. *Dear God,* she prayed silently. *Let this be a dream.*

Across the room that man, that horrifying phantom from the past, knelt down to gaze at her beloved child as if regarding a small god. In a blatant display of mutual veneration, Bobby focused on his newly discovered father with an expression of utter adulation that quite frankly drove a stake through Chessa's heart.

For over nine years Bobby's happiness had been the driving force of her life. Nothing else had mattered. Chessa had completely devoted herself to meeting her son's emotional and physical needs. She'd thought it had been enough. It hadn't.

That hurt.

There was more, so much more. Bobby didn't understand, couldn't understand, that what he clearly believed to be the happiest moment of his life was in reality the worst thing that could possibly have happened. The joy in his young eyes would soon be replaced by pain and loathing. Chessa couldn't allow that to happen but didn't know how to stop it.

With a choked cry she spun back into the kitchen, staggered to the sink. Bracing herself, she gasped for breath, propped herself against the counter with widespread, trembling arms. Perhaps this was all a hoax, a cruel joke played by an impeccably groomed imposter wearing Italian loafers and a designer suit that probably cost more than her monthly mortgage. After all, the vision of prosperity in her living room bore little resemblance to the angry young man she remembered, the sullen adolescent in low-slung jeans and trademark black T-shirt with the sleeves torn out.

The young Nick Purcell had been wild, rebellious, always on the cutting edge of trouble, with a doleful James Dean sex appeal that teenage girls had found irresistible. He'd been the subject of gossip, whispers, speculation, and had been rumored to enjoy a love life more active than a rock musician.

Every town had at least one bad boy. The central California farming community where Chessa grew up had more than its share, although Nick Purcell had been far and away the most notorious. It was in the blood, folks had said. Like father, like son.

Like father. Like son.

"Chessa?"

She spun around, faced him with terror in her heart. Her chest heaved as she struggled for air. She blinked rapidly. The image did not disappear.

He was there. He was real.

Extending a hand, Nick started to speak, then dropped his arm to his side with an anguished expression. His gaze flickered around the neat kitchen to settle on the plate of half-eaten pizza on the table. He smiled. "Sausage and mushroom," he murmured. "It's my favorite, too."

Chessa found her voice. "Why are you here?"

The smile faded, tucked itself back into a face that was stronger than she remembered, but just as handsome. A square jaw. Perfect nose. Lips that were both virile and vulnerable, and dark eyes beneath a swath of brow that gave him a uniquely brooding appearance.

His sigh was nearly imperceptible, more sad than impatient. "I had to see him."

She closed her eyes, clamped her lips together. This wasn't happening. It wasn't.

Pivoting around, she snatched a paring knife off the counter, grabbed an apple and carved frantically. "You had no right to come here."

"He's my son."

Breath caught in her throat. She closed her eyes, bit her lip, then refilled her lungs and dug the paring

knife into the pale fruit flesh to shape the bridge of
the nose, the gouge of a mouth. "Bobby is my son,
not yours."

A moment of silence. When Nick spoke again, she
realized he'd moved closer to her. "I don't blame
you for being angry. I should have been there for
you. I'm sorry I wasn't."

The knife hovered over the partially carved apple.
She chanced a glance over her shoulder, regretted it
instantly. The expression on his face was one of guilt
and torment.

He covered his pain quickly, clasping his hands
behind his back the way a powerful man does to
display command of an uncomfortable situation. "I
wish you'd been able to tell me about our child. Of
course, I understand why you couldn't."

Caution deadened her voice into a dull monotone.
"Precisely what is it that you understand, Mr. Purcell?"

Raising his chin a notch, he twisted his mouth in
a type of a shrug. "Calculating back from the date
of Bobby's birth, I realize that I'd already left town
before you could possibly have known you were
pregnant."

She couldn't have been more shocked if he'd
punched her. "How do you know when Bobby was
born?"

Apparently baffled by the question, he retrieved a
folded sheet from his breast pocket, stepped forward
to display it.

A moment before the room started to spin, Chessa
recognized the copy of her son's birth certificate.
Without realizing that she still held the paring knife,

she absently clasped her trembling hands, oblivious to the sting until Nick sprang forward.

"You've cut yourself." Alarmed, he dropped the document, pried the paring knife from her hand, then snatched a tea towel from the counter and pressed it to the superficial wound. His touch was warm, firm, exquisitely gentle. "Do you have any bandages?"

"That isn't necessary." She pulled away, feeling strange. "I'd like you to leave now."

A peculiar sadness shadowed his gaze. "You know I can't do that."

"Of course you can. You're good at leaving."

The snap in her voice jarred him. He stepped back, regarding her with unnerving intensity. "I understand how you feel."

"No, you don't." She hated the frantic quaver in her voice, the high-pitched hysteria hovering at the back of her throat. "You can't possibly understand. Please, please, I'm begging you, just go away and leave us alone."

His eyelids fluttered shut, and she saw a scrape of white as his teeth grazed his lower lip. A shudder moved through him. When he opened his eyes, he regarded her with a peculiar hesitance. "Chessa, you have every right to be hurt, and to feel abandoned. I want to make that up to you."

"You can't."

"I can try." As she tried to turn away, he touched her arm, and the warmth radiated from his fingers like a small flame. "I want you to know that—" he paused for breath "—that you were always special to me."

Chessa stiffened. "Excuse me?"

He licked his lips, tried for a smile that didn't quite

make it. "What we had together, what we shared was very special."

All she could do was stare at him in utter awe. How gallant of him, she thought, to fake memories that didn't exist about a relationship that never happened. Until five minutes ago, Chessa Margolis and Nick Purcell had never even met.

Chapter Two

During the few minutes it took for Chessa to retrieve an adhesive strip and bandage her hand, her mind was in chaos. There was no easy escape from the tangle of lies. Truth was the only option now, a truth that would deeply disappoint the son she adored. Postponing the inevitable would only intensify his disillusionment.

There was no choice, of course. Chessa knew that, and gathered her courage for what was to come. A deep breath, a silent prayer, and she faced the stranger in her kitchen. "We have to talk."

Nick glanced up. "Isn't it easier just to slice them?"

"Slice them?" She followed his gaze to the partially sculpted fruit draining on a paper towel. "Oh, the apples aren't for pie. I sculpt them into novelty dolls as part of my craft business. Creations by Chessa." To her horror, high-pitched laughter bubbled off a tongue quite clearly out of control. "It's not a big business, of course. Just spare time. I make wreaths out of dried foliage, too. And holiday decorations, of course.''

"I see.'' Clearly he didn't see at all, although a distinctly amused glint lightened an otherwise dark gaze. "Are all of your apple faces as grumpy as this one?''

A glance at the sculpture in question revealed deep-set eyes beneath a slash of intense brow, a slightly imperfect nose above a mouth more detailed and exquisitely carnal than any she'd sculpted before. It was without doubt the scowling, apple-carved equivalent of Nick Purcell himself.

"Are you all right?''

Her head snapped around. "Of course." She took a step back, her gaze darting to the window beyond which her excited son was telling every child in the neighborhood about his newly discovered father. A wave of nausea folded her forward.

"You're ill.'' Instantly concerned, Nick helped her to a chair, brought her a glass of water, then seated himself across the table from her.

She sipped the water, keeping her eyes closed until the sickness passed.

"Are you pregnant?''

Her eyelids snapped open. "I beg your pardon?''

"I'm sorry.'' Having the grace to look embarrassed, he pushed away Bobby's plate of half-eaten pizza and heaved a strained sigh. "It's none of my business—''

"You're right, it's none of your business, I am none of your business, and my son is none of your business.''

"That's where you're wrong.'' Although his voice

was mild, a bolt of danger erupted, displayed by the subtle clench of his jaw, the warning twitch of his mouth. "Bobby is also my son. That makes him my business." A flash of anger, a striking image of defiance and danger that, for a fleeting moment, echoed the passion of his youth.

Then he blinked and it was gone, replaced by the circumspect comprehension of a man experienced in exercising absolute dominion over his own emotions. He adjusted his cuffs, a gesture Chessa perceived as a delaying tactic by one who disliked losing control.

Feeling hollow inside, she twirled the glass between her palms. "This has all been a terrible mistake." She barely recognized the guttural croak as her own voice. "It's my fault, of course. I don't expect you to forgive me, but I have to explain—" She gasped as Nick reached across the table to cup his hands around hers, squeezing them between the warmth of his palms and the coolness of the glass. His touch was firm yet tender, so warm that the heat radiated up her arm to tingle at the pulse in her throat.

Compassion softened his features. Regret clouded his eyes. "I'm the one who begs forgiveness. If I'd known, if I'd realized that—" he paused, clearly confused and struggling for words "—that our time together had resulted in a child, I never would have left. You must believe that."

Groaning, Chessa could only shake her head. "No, no, you don't understand."

"Yes, I do," he insisted, and confirmed that by squeezing her hands. "That was a foolish time in my life. I did things I'm not proud of, things I deeply regret. I was angry and impulsive, resentful of those who had the kind of family life that I could only dream about. I acted out what was expected of me. It was all I knew at the time, all that I'd been taught."

A poignant ache spread behind Chessa's ribs. Memories flooded back, rich and textured, the distant image of a sad young man with no joy in his eyes, the lonely adolescent who'd become a man long before he was ready.

Everyone in town had known Nick as Crazy Lou's kid. According to local lore, Lou Purcell had always been down on his luck, a less-than-ambitious fellow who'd tried to support his family with a variety of jobs that for one reason or another had never worked out. When his wife died, Lou stopped trying and started drinking. Chessa thought Nick had been about twelve at the time.

Pitied at first, the bereaved youngster had been subjected to whispered speculation about bruises he couldn't hide, the constant hunger in his eyes. Over the years, Nick had grown taller, angrier, wilder. Eventually town gossip turned from sympathy to condemnation. The apple doesn't fall far from the tree. Rotten to the core. Like father, like son.

From Chessa's perspective, Nick had done everything humanly possible to prove them right. He'd hung with a rough crowd, faced his detractors with swaggering bravado and garnered a reputation for never turning his back on a fight.

For some reason, girls adored him. At the time, Chessa hadn't understood the attraction. He'd been handsome enough, but there was always an aura of danger about him that she'd found personally offputting. They'd never spoken to each other. She doubted he'd even noticed her. It hadn't been difficult to keep her distance, since he'd been two years ahead of her in school. Even so, most of her female classmates swooned whenever the town bad boy sauntered past, and by the time he was a senior in high school, townsfolk had been willing to believe any sordid story attributed to him, no matter how skimpy the source.

When he finally skipped town one step ahead of the law, most folks said good riddance, and presumed they'd seen the last of Nick Purcell.

Which is exactly why his name had been chosen for her son's birth certificate. Now Chessa had to explain it to him. She didn't have a clue how that could be done, particularly since she barely understood it herself.

"Mr. Purcell," she began, amending it when he hiked a brow. "Nick." She swallowed, extracted her hands from beneath his and folded them in her lap. "I made a terrible mistake ten years ago, and I regret it." The shock in his eyes stung her. She quickly looked away. "I never meant for you to be involved in this."

His gaze narrowed. "In other words, you never meant for me to know about my own son."

Shaking her head, she sighed, pinched the bridge of her nose. God, this was difficult. "Bobby is not—"

An envelope was dropped on the table, an envelope with Nick's name printed in an all-too-familiar childish scrawl.

Stunned, she straightened, staring at the item as if it were a ticking bomb. "What is this?"

"Read it."

Every fiber of intuition in her body forbade her to do so. She didn't want to know what was inside, didn't want to open this paper Pandora's box that she instinctively realized would turn her life, and the life of her son, completely upside down.

It was too late for caution. Nick Purcell was here. Their lives had already been irreversibly altered. All she could do now was minimize the damage. Perhaps the contents of this envelope held a clue as to how she could do that.

Trembling, she extracted a folded sheet of lined paper. One edge was ragged with circular tatters, as if torn from one of the spiral notebooks Bobby favored for his schoolwork. She carefully opened the letter and started to read:

Dear Dad
Hi. My name is Bobby. I'm your son. I don't know how come you never come visit me. I figured maybe it is because you don't know where I am.
The reason I am writing you is because my school is going to have a father-son picnic next month. It will be real fun if you can come. If you don't want to, that is okay, but I don't want to borrow other people's dads anymore so I will just watch TV. We have a real cool TV. Mom bought it last year. It is not very big, but I like it anyway.
I think about you all the time. What do you look like? Are you real tall? Do you like to play soccer? Mom promised she would tell me all about you when I got big. I am big now. I wish she would tell me, but it makes her sad.

I hope you can come to the picnic. I love you.

Your son, Bobby Margolis

Their address and phone number had been carefully printed at the bottom of the page.

Moisture gathered in Chessa's eyes, blurring the lines. "Where did you get this?"

"It was couriered to me from a San Francisco law firm, along with a copy of Bobby's birth certificate."

"San Francisco? I don't understand."

"Neither did I." He leaned back, regarding her thoughtfully. "So I called the law firm and spoke to Bobby's lawyer."

"Bobby doesn't have a lawyer."

"Oh, but he does. One Clementine Allister St. Ives, Esq. She claims Bobby has put her on retainer to handle his affairs. Don't worry," he added when Chessa's jaw dropped in disbelief. "I've checked it out. Ms. St. Ives is quite legitimate, a highly regarded family-law attorney with a fine reputation in the community."

Chessa pushed away from the table. "This is madness. My son is nine years old, for heaven's sake. He doesn't need an attorney, he doesn't have any 'affairs' to handle, and he's never even been to San Fran—" the memory of a recent school outing popped into her mind "—cisco," she finished lamely. "Good grief. His class museum trip."

"Apparently." Tucking the letter back into his pocket, Nick relayed what he'd learned about how Bobby had sneaked away from his classmates, taken a cab to Clementine's office and hired her to find the man whose name graced his birth certificate.

With every word Chessa's heart sank lower in her

chest. Over the years she'd pushed the memories away, always believing she'd never have to face what she'd done, what she'd been forced to do. She'd thought her son was happy, that the life she'd struggled to create for him had been enough.

It hadn't been enough. The pain and loss expressed in his letter had proven that. How could she tell her son that the father he'd searched for, the father he'd dreamed about all his young life, didn't even exist? Tears swelled, spilled down her cheeks. She couldn't stop them.

"Chessa, please, don't cry. It's all right." Reaching across the table, Nick slipped his thumb beneath her chin, a touch so gentle it made her heart ache. "You don't have to do this alone anymore. I'm here now. I can help."

Her breath backed into her throat, nearly choking her. There was something miraculous in his eyes, a poignancy and compassion the depth of which she'd never seen. It soothed her, comforted her, made her feel as if everything might be all right after all. It wouldn't be, of course. It couldn't be. But at that moment Chessa wanted desperately to believe.

A jarring slam broke into her reverie. "Dad, Dad!" Muffled thuds shook the living room floor as a dozen sneakered feet stomped into the house. Bobby skidded into the kitchen, followed by a sweating group of his buddies. "Dad, Dad, Danny wants to see your gun!"

"Gun?" Chessa's head snapped around. "What gun?"

Nick, too, seemed perplexed. "I don't own a gun."

Crushed, Bobby avoided Danny's smug grin. "But I thought private investigators always carried guns."

"I'm not a private investigator, son." Smiling, he shifted in his chair, laid a paternal hand on the boy's shoulder. "I own a private security business. We install alarm systems, communication equipment, that kind of thing."

"Oh." Clearly disappointed, the child managed a brave shrug. "That's kinda cool, I guess." He brightened. "Do you like to play soccer? You wanna come outside and see my bike? There's a really neat park down the street. You wanna go there? And Danny's got a swell dog. He knows how to shake hands and roll over and everything. We could play with him, if you want. Oh!" Bobby grabbed Nick's hand, half hauled him to his feet. "You've gotta come up and look at my room! I've got all kinds of neat car models and some airplanes. Do you like *Star Wars?* I've got a real Jedi Knight light saber!"

Before Nick could respond, he was surrounded by the gaggle of chattering children and hustled away. A moment later the front door slammed again. The house fell into eerie silence. Chessa was alone. Alone with her fears, alone with her memories, alone with the crushing guilt.

"I know about the bid opening tomorrow morning, Roger. I'll be there." Shifting the cellular phone, Nick paced around the sofa in Chessa's small living room, using his free hand to riffle through his appointment book. "Have my secretary reschedule all appointments to end by two o'clock on Tuesdays and Thursdays for the next ten weeks."

"Impossible." Roger Barlow's voice was thin and

strained, as always, and high-pitched with the stress of being second in command for a business growing faster than a paranoid pragmatist could comfortably handle. "We're meeting with the CEO of National Technologies on Thursday to pitch a marketing strategy for outfitting their corporate headquarters and three satellite manufacturing facilities. That contract could be worth a half million dollars. We can't reschedule."

Barlow was a good man, with a by-the-book persona that provided needed balance to his own loosely creative management style. His constant whining was irritating, but Nick respected his business acumen. "If it can't be rescheduled, you'll have to handle the meeting yourself."

"Me?" The poor man's voice squeaked like a rusty hinge. "I don't know a surveillance cam from a zonal keypad. I'm only a lowly finance director. You're the technology guru. Without you, there is no meeting."

That was true. Nick had always been good with electronics, he had put himself through college installing alarm systems designed by others. Now he designed his own systems and had built a successful company from the ground up.

"Okay, fine. Cancel the meeting."

"Cancel it? Have you lost your mind? What in hell could be more important that a half-million-dollar contract?"

"Soccer."

The poor man sputtered as if he'd swallowed a peach pit, but Nick was distracted by voices upstairs, where Chessa was explaining that Bobby couldn't stay up any later because it was a school night. The frustrated boy was pleading his case, quite eloquently at that, insisting it wasn't every day a kid got to meet his very own father.

Nick's chest tightened. He was suddenly impatient with Roger's nattering on about meetings and money as if there was nothing more important on earth. A week ago Nick might have agreed with that. Today he knew better.

Today he was standing in a home filled with odd bric-a-brac, decorative crafts and unique furnishings that would have appeared garish in less-talented hands. Chessa clearly had a knack for creating character out of chaos. A giant cable spool had been turned into a telephone table from which huge, dried flowers bristled in an oddly appropriate wilderness bouquet. Coats by the front door dangled from the plywood antlers of a Bullwinkle cartoon character, five feet high and lacquered in primary colors bright enough to make the eyes bleed.

An olive-green sideboard stenciled with Dutch designs towered beside a brocade sofa spruced up with embroidered throw pillows and a draped afghan, studded by riotous cartoon characters. Every space on the wall was filled with twisted wreaths of dried twigs and flowers, puffy quilt miniatures trimmed with handmade lace, and peculiar garage-sale items like gigantic carved salad tongs, eighteenth-century bedwarmers and a rusted wagon wheel studded with spears of dried lavender and windflowers.

And of course there were photographs. Dozens of them, set proudly on the spool telephone table, the green sideboard, an iron plant stand that had been converted to a knickknack shelf, and dotting the walls—all lovingly framed with handmade lace or tucked into a nest of braided twigs.

Every photograph was of Bobby. Bobby as an infant, as a drooling toddler, as a grinning first-grader with no front teeth. Bobby in a football jersey. Bobby at the beach. Bobby throwing a snowball. School portraits, candid snapshots, year after year of his son's life captured in pictures.

Nick had already missed all those years. He wouldn't miss any more.

Closing the appointment book, he tucked it back into his pocket, interrupting Roger's sniveled protest with a tone that brooked no argument. "I've agreed to assist my son's soccer coach. The team practices on Tuesdays and Thursdays. I'll be unavailable on those afternoons for the duration of the season. As for the National Technologies meeting, you can either reschedule it, cancel it or handle it alone. You decide."

"But—"

"I'll be in the office tomorrow morning. We'll discuss it then."

The poor man sounded apoplectic. "But what about the fish?"

"Fish?"

"There's a goldfish in the water cooler."

"Oh, that fish." Nick chuckled, having nearly forgotten what was bound to have been one of his most memorable pranks. "Is the fish in question causing any distress?"

"Er, well, Ms. Pipps from Accounting is quite troubled. She won't drink the water, of course. No one will."

That came as no surprise, although the cooler had

been disabled lest an unobservant soul attempted to use the converted fish tank for its original purpose. "You'll find several cases of imported spring water in the lunch room. Oh, and there's a box of fish food on my desk."

"Fish food?"

"Just a pinch, Roger. Mustn't overfeed, you know." With that, Nick thumbed the cell phone off, folded it into his jacket pocket, and focused his attention on the soft footsteps descending the stairs. He knew it was Chessa. There was a distinctive pattern to her movement, a delicate rhythm to her step.

Over the past few hours he'd studied everything about her, from the timid smile that she offered too rarely to the way her eyes widened when she was taken by surprise, as she had been when Bobby had insisted Nick stay for dinner. He'd recognized her anxiety and felt guilty about not having graciously extricated himself from the situation.

The truth was that he'd wanted to stay, had wanted to continue his study of this intriguing woman with the haunted eyes. Everything about her fascinated him, even her unique manner of wielding a dinner fork as if it were something regal. Nick had pieced every mannerism into his memory, searching for something, anything that would jog him into recalling details of their past together. The image remained elusive, a fleeting ghost from a past he'd escaped long ago and the memories he'd left behind.

Halfway down the stairs, Chessa paused when she saw him, gripped the varnished oak banister so tightly that even from his vantage point in the living room, Nick could see her fingers whiten.

She moistened her lips, regarded him with thinly

disguised disapproval. "Bobby would like to say good-night to you." Avoiding his gaze, she descended the final steps and crossed the living room without so much as a glance in his direction. "Please leave his bedroom door open and turn the hall light on when you're through. Bobby is afraid of the dark."

With that she disappeared into the kitchen. Nick went to say good-night to his son.

Thirty minutes later Nick came downstairs just as Chessa emerged from the kitchen carrying a flat sheet of carved apples. Her eyes widened a moment, but she recovered quickly and swished past him as if unaffected by his presence. "I was beginning to wonder if you'd forgotten how to get downstairs."

He stepped around the old steamer trunk that enhanced the eclectic decor by serving as a coffee table. "Bobby is a very verbal young man," he said. There seemed no reason to explain that he'd spent the past half hour explaining why refusal to move into their guest room didn't mean he wasn't going to be a part of his life. Not that the idea didn't hold a certain appeal, although it didn't take a psychic to realize that Chessa would be less than amenable to the idea.

Stopping at a closed door behind the stairwell, she propped the flat pan against her hip, freed one hand and opened the door, disappearing inside before Nick could spring forward to assist her.

The hollow sound of footsteps on wooden stairs filtered from the open doorway, along with the occasional creak of old boards strained with age. A light sprayed from the opening, which Nick presumed led to a basement.

Acutely aware that he hadn't been invited to follow, he clasped his hands behind his back, rocked impatiently on the balls of his feet. He glanced at his watch, then back toward the basement door. Sounds filtered up. A clunk, a thunk, a rustling scratch, as if something heavy had been dragged across metal.

It was a two-hour drive back to Marin County. If he left now, he'd make it before midnight.

More scraping from downstairs. Nick sidled toward the doorway, peered down the narrow basement stairs. A low ceiling obstructed his view, so he descended the first few steps. Fluorescent lights flooded the room with brilliant illumination. Two more steps, and he stopped in his tracks, stunned by what he saw.

The huge basement had been transformed into a large assembly bay, with supply bins and long counters heaped with fabric. Sheaths of dried weeds and flowers hung from the rafters, and one section was a mailing area, complete with stacks of boxes, tapes and labels. "Good grief," he mumbled. "You've got quite an operation down here."

Startled, Chessa leaped away from the large dehydrator into which she'd been arranging the carved apples, touched her throat, then sagged against the counter.

"I didn't mean to frighten you." Continuing down the steps, Nick glanced around the room, noticing an old sewing machine on a counter heaped with bolts of cloth, and bins of what appeared to be tiny doll clothes. "You actually sell these things?"

"Yes." Across the room, Chessa completed loading the apples without embellishment. She'd been quiet all day and apparently wasn't feeling any more talkative now.

Nick sauntered past the mailing area, glancing at a few of the packed boxes, which had been neatly labeled to specialty stores around the country. "A nationwide clientele? I'm impressed."

She closed the door, crossed her arms and regarded him warily. "Is there something I can do for you?"

Puffing his cheeks, Nick blew out a breath and jammed his hands in his slacks pockets. "I didn't mean to intrude. You left the basement door open, so I presumed you didn't mind if I joined you."

"I always leave the door open so I can hear Bobby." Her gaze skittered away, settled on a spot in thin air. "He sometimes wakes up during the night."

"Nightmares?"

"No, not really. He just wants to make certain I'm here."

Nick regarded a nervous twitch at the corner of her mouth. "Has he ever awakened and not found you here?"

The nervous twitch hardened into a flat, angry line. "I have always been here for my son," she snapped. "How dare you imply otherwise?"

He managed to stifle a groan of regret at having uttered such an asinine and insensitive comment. "I'm sorry. Of course you have. We both know that I'm the one who hasn't been here. I can't change the past. I'm here now, and I intend to be part of my son's life from this day forward."

Every trace of color drained from her face. She swayed slightly, and for a moment Nick feared her knees might buckle. As he reached out, she stiffened, held out a hand like a shield. Since she appeared ready to bolt, he dropped his hands to his side and stepped back, giving her space.

She took one deep breath, then another. When she finally met his gaze, her expression was steel hard and determined. "I realize you've been put in an untenable position, Mr. Purcell, and I deeply regret it. Please understand that none of this is your fault, but my son is my first and only priority. The longer this goes on, the more deeply he will be hurt. I don't want you to be a part of his life. In fact, I don't want you to see him again. Ever."

For a moment Nick simply stared at her. "I'm sorry you feel that way."

Her chest deflated slightly, as if she'd exhaled all her air at once. The relief in her eyes stung. "I'm the one who is sorry. You've been very kind to Bobby, and I appreciate it. I would also appreciate you respecting my wishes."

"I do respect your wishes. Unfortunately I cannot and will not honor them."

Comprehension dawned slowly in her eyes, which widened from disbelief into an appealing combination of anger and indignation. "Perhaps you didn't understand. I do not want you to have any further contact with my son."

"I understand perfectly." Nick, too, was growing angry. "But I've already been denied nine years of my son's life. I have no intention of being denied any more of it."

"Bobby is not your son!" The words were shrill and sharp, shockingly so. Recovering quickly, she clasped her hands, hiked her chin with royal dignity. "I've already apologized. I don't know what else to do. I never meant for you to become involved in this.

Never in my wildest dreams could I have imagined—'' Biting her lower lip, she struggled for control. She crossed her arms, hugging herself. "Please, just leave us alone."

Inside, Chessa was shaking so violently she feared she might collapse.

Bobby is not your son.

She'd said it. The words were out. There was nothing she could do to make amends to Nick Purcell for all that she'd put him through, but he seemed a strong man, and despite his shaky start in life, she believed he was a good man, as well. Eventually she would try to explain what had happened. Maybe he'd understand; maybe he wouldn't. Either way Nick Purcell had always been a survivor.

Bobby was another matter. Her beloved child had wrapped all his hopes and dreams around this man, hopes and dreams that his own mother hadn't even recognized. Chessa would carve out her own heart to avoid hurting her son, but there seemed no way to avoid it now. For a brief and shining moment, he'd had a dad of his own. Now she had to take that away from him.

He would hate her for it.

Footsteps snapped across the concrete floor, catching her attention. Nick Purcell was leaving. A rush of relief was tempered by a peculiar sense of loss. She wasted no time analyzing that. An interminable night stretched before her, an agonizing night during which she must decide the gentlest way to break her son's heart.

At the base of the stairs Nick stopped abruptly. "I'll be here Tuesday afternoon around four. Please inform my son that I'll meet him at the soccer field, as planned.''

Nick had moved halfway up the stairs before Chessa found her voice. "Wait!"

He favored her with a cool look. "Yes?"

"Didn't you hear what I said?"

"I heard you."

"Bobby is not your son."

"This says that he is," Nick replied, patting the breast pocket into which he'd slipped the copy of Bobby's birth certificate. "You've done a fine job raising our child, Chessa. After all these years, I can understand why you wouldn't be pleased by the prospect of sharing him. But share him you will, or our lawyers will meet in court and the truth will be laid bare.''

The truth. Laid bare. In court, where her son would be devastated by it.

Chessa couldn't let that happen. Not now, not ever.

Nick's gaze burned straight into her soul. "Do we understand each other?''

Somehow she managed to lift her chin a notch to keep it from quivering. "Yes, we understand each other.''

"Tuesday, then. You'll tell him?"

"I'll tell him."

With a curt nod Nick strode up the stairs. A moment later Chessa heard the front door open and close. Only then did she sag against the drying counter and allow the tears to flow.

All these years she'd believed her secret was safe.

She hadn't realized how desperately her son wanted a father, nor could she possibly have imagined how desperately Nick wanted to be one.

There was no choice now. No choice at all.

Chapter Three

Stars above, lights below, brilliantly twinkling and pulsing in the velvet night. A midnight bluff overlooking a sleeping town blurred by fogged windows and the heady scent of love. The car shuddered. Soft moans, sweet breath, shudders of ecstasy.

His body sighed; his mind swirled. A whisper of silken hair, the embrace of soft arms, fragrant with perfume. A veiled face, nebulous and obscure, clouded by passion and the misty muddle of an intoxicated mind.

From somewhere beyond conscious thought, a melody beckoned. A voice, fresh and lyrical, summoned him, rousting his mind from pleasures of the flesh to something deeper, more poignant. Sweet arms held him, a gentle whisper begged him not to look. He had to look, had to lay eyes upon the vision from which such mellifluous beauty could emerge.

Condensation mysteriously evaporated, revealing a circle of clarity on the cloudy glass. A face floated in the darkness, a face of such stunning beauty that he was paralyzed by its intensity. Sable hair, ruffled by an invisible breeze. Eyes blue enough to blind a man with radiance. Dewy lips, lush and alluring, set in a regal face of such dignity that he was humbled in its presence.

It was her, he realized. It had always been her.

Nick bolted upright, sweating, heart pounding, mind struggling to emerge from the netherworld of sleep. Breath came in shallow gulps. His limbs trembled. His eyes burned.

Stumbling from his darkened bedroom, he padded into the kitchen and drank a quart of orange juice straight from the carton. His mind cleared slowly, but remnants of the dream remained.

Eyes that pierce the soul and haunt a man's dreams. A captivating smile, a beguiling voice, a face no man could ever forget. She had come to him tonight, had invaded his mind, guided him back to that precious moment in time when they had created a life together.

There was no doubt now, no doubt at all.

"What are you doing here?" Clearly surprised by the unexpected visit, Marjorie Margolis made no move to open the screen door, to hug her daughter or offer any other gesture of affection. A small dog dashed about the woman's ankles, yapping madly. "Aren't you supposed to be at work? Oh, God." Touching her throat, Marjorie narrowed her gaze into the familiar expression of disappointment and reproach that had haunted Chessa's childhood. "You've lost your job, haven't you? If you need money—"

"It's nice to see you, too, Mother."

Marjorie clamped her lips together and drew her round shoulders up. "You needn't be snippy, Chessa. It's been months since you've favored us with your presence. I suppose a thirty-minute drive is far too daunting for such a busy person as yourself."

"The roads run both ways, Mother." Sighing, Chessa rubbed her eyelids. This had been a mistake. She should have known better. Whenever Chessa and her mother were in the same room, tension was sharp enough to sting, and words became weapons. If not for Bobby, Chessa probably wouldn't have had any relationship with her parents beyond greeting cards and a Christmas phone call. As it was, they saw each other only a few times each year, on holidays and Bobby's birthday.

To their credit, Chessa's parents adored their only grandchild. The feeling was mutual. Bobby incessantly bragged about his gramma and grampa as if he was the only child on earth to have grandparents. Family had always been important to Bobby, which is why Chessa struggled to maintain a strained relationship with the parents whose long-ago betrayal still wounded her.

Marjorie stood stiffly, clasping her puffy hands, continuing to ignore the yipping terrier bouncing like a hairy Ping-Pong ball behind the closed screen door. Chessa turned to leave, paused at the click of a latch.

"You might as well come in." Her mother's brusque tone held the slightest quaver of supplication.

For a moment Chessa was tempted to refuse. Only the urgency of her mission compelled her to enter the familiar house in which she'd evolved from wide-eyed innocent to pragmatic adult.

As she stepped into the living room, the tiny animal leaped up to scratch at her knees, a frantic appeal for attention that Chessa could sadly understand. Smiling, she knelt to pet the quivering ball of fur, and was rewarded by a flurry of damp doggie kisses. "Aren't you the sweetest thing?" she crooned, wondering how long her parents had owned a dog. As a child, she hadn't been allowed to have pets.

Above her, Marjorie loomed like a martyred saint. "I have some money put aside," she said quietly. "You're welcome to it, but you mustn't tell your father."

Chessa rose slowly. "I haven't lost my job, Mother. I called in sick."

"You don't seem ill, dear," There was no concern evident in the question, only mild reproach.

"I'm not."

"So you lied?"

A cluck of disapproval tightened Chessa's stomach at the same time her mother's hypocrisy steamed in her blood. Lies were at the heart of their family, the foundation upon which more lies had been heaped until the truth had been lost in a twisted web of deception.

Marjorie cleared her throat, wrung her hands with more fervor. "In that case, to what do I owe the honor of this visit?"

"We have to talk, Mother."

"A telephone was inadequate for that purpose?"

The reminder that she could have called made Chessa flinch, although the thought hadn't even occurred to her until this moment. She'd found herself driven by instinct, a primal need for personal contact that made no sense given their sad history. "I wanted to see you."

"Oh?" Marjorie's eyes softened, grew moist. For a moment a hint of the compassion she'd once bestowed freely emerged, reminding Chessa of happier days when her mother had held her and hugged her and loved her with all the maternal devotion any child could want.

It had all been so long ago. Chessa hadn't realized how much she missed it.

In the blink of an eye the moment passed and Marjorie reined in her emotion, nodding toward the sparkling, unwrinkled sofa with an expansive, hostesslike gesture. "Please, make yourself comfortable, dear. I haven't been shopping today, but I believe I have some tea cakes and—"

"Nick Purcell is back," Chessa blurted out, and watched her mother's already-pale complexion blanch to a sickly white. "He knows about Bobby."

Marjorie swayed once, gripped the arm of a burgundy velour wing chair and seated herself slowly. Her lips moved silently. She moistened them with her tongue. "How?"

Chessa couldn't reply immediately. A tremor moved up from the base of her spine, split at her shoulders and traveled the length of her arms. Her hands began to shake. "It's a long story."

The older woman braced herself, fitting her plump body to the stiff-backed chair, clasping white fingers into a death knot on her lap. Sunlight streamed from a living-room window, glinting on the gold watchband choking her swollen wrist, highlighting faded strands of drab gray-brown hair twisted into a loose bun at her crown. A jawline once as clean and sharp as Chessa's was now squared with age; puffy envelopes of purplish skin sagged beneath eyes that retained the crystal blue of her youth—the same color and clarity as those of her daughter and grandson.

Marjorie shuddered a breath. "Tell me."

Gathering her courage, Chessa perched on the pristine sofa and spent the next twenty minutes explaining how Bobby had found a copy of his birth certificate, then sneaked away from his class outing, hired a lawyer and sought out the man he'd believed to be his father. As she spoke, her voice faltered and her mother's eyes glazed with fear.

There were reasons for that fear, reasons that few people on earth understood. Two of those who knew had left the country years ago; two of them were in this room. That left only Jacqueline Shane, Chessa's high-school confidante, who'd married and moved far away, and Chessa's father, the instigator of this sordid tragedy, who was away at work.

For that, at least, Chessa was grateful. If her relationship with her mother was tenuous, her relationship with the father she'd once adored was practically nonexistent.

It wasn't a lack of love that had broken the father-daughter bond. It was a lack of trust. James Margolis had betrayed Chessa, and he knew it. From the day of Bobby's birth, he'd never been able to meet his daughter's eyes. Guilt, Chessa supposed, a guilt she secretly shared. She, too, had betrayed a child. Complicity in her father's lie had assured that. Both betrayals had now come home to roost.

"Your father did what had to be done," Marjorie

said as if reading her mind. "He was protecting you."

"He was protecting himself," Chessa snapped back, knowing the accusation was as unfair as it was true. James Margolis had caved in to pressure to save his career, and in doing so, he'd saved his family's livelihood.

As a shattered sixteen-year-old, Chessa hadn't understood. After nearly a decade of financial struggle to raise her own son, she now had a glimmer of the panic her father must have felt when Eugene Carlyle, owner of the largest employer in town, had given him an edict few men would have had the courage to refuse.

It had been nearly ten years ago—the end of an oppressively hot summer that marked the final season of her youth and heralded her entrance into a grown-up world for which she'd been woefully unprepared.

Chessa could still remember the sickly sweet smell of flowers in the stately drawing room of the Carlyle mansion. Every detail of that terrible night was indelibly etched in her memory. The frantic pinch of young Anthony Carlyle's fingers squeezing her hand; the fury raging in the elder Carlyle's eyes, while Anthony's mother twisted her prim lips in disgust, a stark contrast to Marjorie's downcast expression of shame and James's meek acquiescence.

It had been a night of shock and revelation. No one disputed that Anthony Carlyle had fathered Chessa's child. Anthony and Chessa were as deeply in love as two young hearts could possibly be. Anthony had been stunned by Chessa's pregnancy, but had promised to stand by her. In her romanticized young mind, that meant only one thing: marriage.

Her friend Jacqueline had tried to warn her, had told Chessa the Carlyles would never accept her, would never accept her child. Time had proven her right.

The past faded with the creak of a chair. Across the room Marjorie stood, causing the terrier to leap from its resting spot and rush forth yipping nervously.

Ignoring the worried little animal, Marjorie mumbled as she paced. "It wasn't your father's fault, Chessa. If you would be honest with yourself, you'd realize that he had no choice in the matter." She whirled, her face gray, her eyes sharp with panic. "You were the one who ran out and got pregnant. You created the problem—you and that spoiled little brat you allowed into your bed. You jeopardized everything—your father's career, our family's reputation. My God, we could have been ruined. Your father saved us from all of that. How dare you criticize him? How dare you?"

There was no reasonable reply, of course. Marjorie was right. It had been Chessa who'd fallen in love with the son of Weaverton's most influential citizen, who also happened to be her own father's employer. In retrospect she accepted responsibility for her impulsiveness, although she honestly didn't regret it. Her behavior had been rash, but it had produced a precious child, a son she loved more than life itself.

She could never regret having Bobby. It was the lie she regretted, the one lie that begat another lie, then another and another until the foundation of deceit had become so towering and brittle it threatened to collapse upon all that she held dear.

It had all started a decade ago, with two teenagers

in love, two families in crisis and a meeting to discuss options. At least, that's what Chessa and Anthony had believed at the time. As it turned out, their future and that of their unborn child had already been decided by Eugene Carlyle, and the raft of attorneys he employed.

There had been much pontificating and batting about of legal terminology, but the bottom line had actually been quite simple. If Chessa had publicly named Anthony as the father of her unborn child, James Margolis's employment would have been terminated, and the Carlyles had threatened a lawsuit to prove paternity. Although the elder Carlyle had conceded blood tests would probably prove conclusive, he left no doubt that the Margolis family would be ruthlessly smeared, and the baby would be publicly denounced by the entire Carlyle clan. He'd also warned that if Anthony was foolish enough to choose Chessa and the baby over the wishes of his parents, he would be immediately disinherited.

Anthony had stiffened at the threat. Despite that, despite her best friend's warning, Chessa still hadn't believed her beloved boyfriend would turn his back on her, nor had she believed that his parents could actually be so callous as to deny their own flesh and blood. Only when Anthony had pulled his hand away, refusing to look at her while her own father signed away the inheritance rights of her unborn child, had Chessa recognized the bitter truth. Everyone she loved had betrayed her.

Chessa had never seen Anthony again. He'd transferred to a private school that fall, and when he'd wrapped his Ferrari around a light pole shortly after Bobby's birth, Chessa had grieved, sworn off men forever, then moved to another town and set about raising her son alone. She'd thought her secret was safe. Until now.

She rubbed her eyelids as if the futile gesture could wipe away the sad memories. It couldn't, of course. Nothing could. Now Chessa posed the one question she'd never had the courage to ask. "Mother, why did Daddy put Nick Purcell's name on Bobby's birth certificate?"

Marjorie jerked to a stop, stared at her daughter as if she'd just asked why the sky was blue. "Because of the boy's reputation, of course. No one would question that the offspring of the town drunk had sired an illegitimate child of his own. Besides Nick Purcell was a fugitive by then, long gone and the type who'd most likely end up in prison, anyway. We all thought we'd seen the last of him."

"And you were willing to saddle your grandchild with that kind of legacy?"

Marjorie looked away, but not before Chessa saw the flush of shame stain her cheeks. "Would you have preferred the stigma of 'father unknown'?"

"I would have preferred the truth."

"That wasn't possible."

"It was possible. You and Daddy simply weren't willing to accept the consequence."

"And why should we?" A crimson tide of anger crawled over her chubby neck. "Your father had spent ten years building a career with Carlyle Electronics. Should he have given all that up because of your mistake? Should I have given up my home, my friends, everything I cared about?"

Chessa considered that. "Those things you cared about, Mother, was I ever one of them?"

Color drained from Marjorie's face as quickly as it had arisen. "You know better than to even ask such a question."

Actually, she did know better. Her mother had always been a solemn person, but until Chessa's teenage years, she'd never been unloving. In hindsight, Chessa realized that she had been the one who'd changed most in that time, asserting her independence, pushing away the mother to whom she'd always run in the past. Of course Marjorie had been bewildered and confused. Now that Chessa was herself a parent, she realized how truly unfair that question had been. "I'm sorry, I didn't mean that the way it sounded."

Marjorie's lip quivered. "We did what we had to do."

"I know." She didn't know at all, but realized that further argument was useless. Standing, she retrieved her car keys from her slacks' pocket. "Now it's time for me to undo it."

"What do you mean by that?"

"It's time to tell the truth, Mother."

"No! You can't, Chessa, you can't do that to your father. He's risen to the top of his profession. This could ruin him."

"The Carlyles sold the company after Anthony's death and moved to Europe, Mother. No one has heard from them in years. They have no power over Daddy's job anymore. You know that."

"If word got out about…about…" The words trailed into silence, shattered only by a hiss of sharply indrawn breath. "There's nothing to be gained by dredging up the past, Chessa, and everything to lose. Think about your father. It doesn't matter that the Carlyles are gone. You know what this town is like, Chessa. The gossip alone could destroy his reputation, and his entire career.''

There was enough truth in that to give her pause. ''What about Nick's reputation, Mother?''

''A man like that has no reputation.''

''Mother, weren't you listening to me? We are not discussing a career felon. Nick is a successful businessman now. He's made something out of his life.''

''That's exactly why you can't tell him. My God, Chessa, he could sue us.'' The frantic woman bobbed her head in response to her daughter's stunned stare. ''Yes, yes, he could. He's got the money, he's got the power. A lawsuit would ruin us. Is that what you want? Is that your plan of vengeance, to see your parents as paupers?''

''Of course not,'' Chessa murmured, although her heart was pounding frantically. Her mother's fears were not entirely baseless. If their deception was exposed, Nick Purcell might very well have grounds for legal action, and might just be angry enough to pursue them. Chessa couldn't have blamed him. There was no excuse for what her family had done to him. He'd been terribly wronged.

In spite of a strained relationship with her parents, Chessa still loved them. Ten years ago she'd made a bad choice, one that had hurt them deeply. Another bad choice could devastate them. It was a sobering thought.

''If you don't care about us, what about Bobby?'' Marjorie's voice was high-pitched, thin with terror. ''Are you ready for him to hate you? Because he will, you know. He'll despise all of us. Is that what you want, Chessa, to destroy your parents and lose your son forever?"

A knot wedged in her chest, forcing shallow, painful breaths. Her mother was right. The truth would shatter her son. It would devastate her parents. It would even crush Nick Purcell, who for reasons Chessa didn't understand, was desperate to be a father. Nothing to be gained; everything to lose.

The tangled web tightened. There seemed no escape.

Nick slammed his fist on his desk, cowed his finance manager with a look. "No."

Tugging his collar, Roger Barlow licked his lips, rocked back a step. "It's just a blood test. A tiny pin prick. The boy will barely notice."

"My son is not an imbecile."

"I'm sure the lad is exceptionally bright, which is why he'll understand that paternity must be legally established." Roger's nasal whine grated on Nick's last nerve. "Does the boy even look like you?"

An image popped into Nick's mind, of clear blue eyes, a sharply dimpled chin, a shock of shiny sable hair framing an inquisitive, freckled face. Nick smiled in response to the proud ache squeezing his chest. "Bobby is a beautiful child. He looks just like his mother."

On the guest side of the expansive mahogany desk, a pair of somber eyes blinked behind myopically thick glasses. "I'd be more comfortable with this situation if he looked just like you."

"Your comfort is not required," Nick snapped with more sharpness than he'd intended. Leaning back into a pillow of soft leather, he steepled his fingers. "Tell me, Roger, how would you feel if your father insisted on medical proof you were his son?" The man's Adam's apple bounced sharply. Nick noted that, before continuing to drive his point home. "Would you be hurt, wondering why he was seeking a reason to reject you? And what about your mother, how would you view her in light of your father's obvious belief that there had been other men in her life?" When the finance manager paled and slicked a hand over his balding scalp, Nick nodded. "Exactly. I won't put Bobby through that."

Roger wasn't ready to give up. "That's commendable, of course, but there are other considerations."

"What considerations, Roger?" Narrowing his gaze, Nick took satisfaction in noting a bead of moisture appear along the squirming man's upper lip. "What could possibly be more important than a child's self-esteem?"

"Protection of company assets," he blurted. "You don't even remember this woman. Who's to say that she's not playing you for a fool?"

Cursing himself for having revealed that tidbit of information even to a trusted assistant, Nick rose slowly, maintaining steady eye contact with his blinking second-in-command. "First, I do not appreciate being considered a fool even in speculative fashion."

"I certainly meant no disrespect—"

"Second, the woman in question has done everything but aim a shotgun at my belly to keep me out of my son's life, hardly the behavior of a fraudulent gold digger."

The fact that she'd repeatedly said that Bobby

wasn't his son hadn't fazed Nick in the least. From her perspective a nine-year abandonment had relieved him of paternal rights and responsibilities. Nick disagreed with that, of course, and had a habit of dismissing any opinion that didn't match his own.

And of course there was the dream.

"Third, I now vividly recall the night my son was conceived. If you are under any other impression, you are mistaken."

The final vestige of color drained from Roger's face. He slumped in defeat. "I understand."

"Good. And Roger?"

The man paused. "Yes?"

"Don't forget to feed the goldfish in the water cooler." Swiveling around, Nick feigned interest in the latest inventory report, signaling an end to the meeting. He continued to flip pages without reading them until Roger left his office.

When the door clicked shut, Nick tossed the report aside and concentrated on that long-ago night he'd dreamed about, the night he now believed his son had been conceived.

There had been a school dance that evening, the last social of the school year. Nick and his friends, a rowdy bunch of thugs who, for some reason, he'd admired immensely at the time, had been joyriding in a friend's flame-stenciled Mustang when they'd pulled up in the school parking lot. Music blasted from the gymnasium. Girls hung in giggling groups at the door, eyeing the new arrivals with blatant interest.

Nick had already downed enough beer to be liberally buzzed when someone pulled out a fifth of whisky. They passed it around, hooting from the car as a trio of sweater-clad coeds swung by to check them out. Nick remembered the burning liquor stinging a path down his throat. He remembered his stomach churning and the moon spinning above him.

He didn't recall leaving the parking lot, but at some point they had. Later, he remembered the sweet scent of perfume, and a soft feminine whisper in his ear. Beyond them, the lights of the town flickered like lightning bugs, and the fragrance of summer grass filled his senses. He was vaguely aware of being on the reservoir bluff overlooking the town, a notorious viewpoint where young lovers sought privacy to indulge carnal pleasures.

Carnal pleasure was what Nick remembered about that night. Soft flesh, warm in his arms. Silken hair brushing his bare chest. Sweet breath pulsing against his ear. Town lights spinning in the distance.

Then the moon spiraled like a crazy rocket, an explosion rocked him to the marrow, and his world had gone black.

He'd awakened the following morning, alone in a strange car with a punched ignition. Nick had never stolen a car before. He didn't remember stealing this one, but presumed that he must have. The previous night was little more than a blur of sensation, disjointed images without rhyme or reason.

Abandoning the vehicle, he'd staggered home on foot, only to discover the police had already been there. It was mid-morning, but his father was already drunk, mean drunk. And he was livid, swaying on his boots, waving the half-empty liquor bottle like a sword. "Damn thieving whelp," he'd shouted. "This is the thanks I get for raising you up. Shoulda throwed you out when your mama died. You ain't no son of mine, ain't my blood.''

Nick had stood there, frozen in shock. The father he'd loved, cared for and fought to defend had cast him out of his heart, out of his life, had denied even being his father.

Nick barely felt the bottle whiz past, was vaguely aware of the sting of glass when it shattered against the wall mere inches from his head. Only when Crazy Lou grabbed the whipping strap from the wall did the numbness dissipate. Nick bolted out of the ramshackle house, sprinted through the woods and just kept on running.

Running to escape the past. Running to escape the future. Running to escape the sound of his father's voice echoing in his brain.

You ain't no son of mine. Ain't my blood.

Ten years later, cushioned in supple leather, surrounded by trappings of success beyond his wildest dreams, those words still haunted him. The rejection. The abandonment. The pain.

From that day forward, Nick had been on his own. His travels had begun down a rocky road of petty crimes to feed himself, and might have ended tragically if not for the guidance of a juvenile detention officer who'd taken an interest in him. He'd been a kind man, the first person in Nick's life who believed he didn't have to be a failure. Nick set out to prove it, pursuing success with single-minded vengeance. His belly still knotted at the memory, his heart still ached at the loss of the father whose approval he'd always craved. So he stoically avoided thoughts of the past just as he'd stoically avoided emotional entanglements and romantic involvements. Work was

Nick's life. It was safe. It was comfortable. He could control it.

Now everything was changing again, making it more difficult to keep his emotions at bay. Nick had never pictured himself as a father. He'd never imagined himself as part of a family, never looked beyond the veneer of financial success he'd created to reconcile the heartbreak of his childhood, a heartbreak he now saw reflected in the eyes of his own child. This lonely boy needed him, needed the caring and guidance of someone who'd been there, who understood what he was going through. Nick could offer that understanding. He could offer the same guidance to his own son that a kindly mentor had once offered to him. For nine years Bobby had been desperate for the father who hadn't been there for him. Nick was determined to make up for that.

God help anyone who got in his way.

"He's here!" Bobby hollered as Chessa drove into the soccer field parking lot. "Dad's here!"

"So he is." She'd barely flipped off the ignition when her son bolted from the car and dashed across the field where dozens of youngsters and parents prepared for team practice. Legs churning, gangly arms flapping like the wings of an awkward goose, Bobby swerved around his teammates and skidded to a stop in front of the beaming man.

Feeling like she'd swallowed a brick, Chessa exited the car, shaded her eyes and watched the interaction between her son and the man he believed to be his father. They were so clearly engrossed in conversation that neither seemed aware of their surroundings. Although too far away to hear the conversation, she could see Bobby chattering madly while Nick hung on every word as if the boy was revealing secrets of the universe.

Then Nick laughed, said something and reached into a nearby duffel to retrieve what appeared to be a small department store bag. Bobby clapped his hands and threw himself against Nick for a hug. Snatching the bag, Bobby headed toward the small green building that housed the park rest room. Only then did Nick refocus his attention, scanning the crowd until his gaze found Chessa, still hovering beside her parked vehicle.

Her heart jumped when their eyes met. Breath backed up in her throat, and her knees wobbled. She told herself it was nerves, a normal reaction to one so saddled by guilt she felt like a whipped mare "ridden hard and put away wet," as her rancher grandpa used to say. A sudden dryness inside her mouth annoyed her.

She swallowed, hiked her chin and pasted a nonchalant expression on her face as Nick worked his way toward her.

His shadow touched her first, along with a pleasant coolness. His smile dazzled her, dizzied her. "Hello, Chessa. It's nice to see you again."

"Yes," she murmured foolishly. "It is." A deep rumble shocked her. She recognized his laughter at the same moment she realized what she'd said. "I mean, it's nice to see you again, too."

Lord what a magnificent smile he had. "Are you staying for practice?"

"Yes." She wasn't about to leave her son alone with a stranger. "How was your trip in from the coast?"

"Fine, thanks. Traffic is light this early in the afternoon." He rocked back on his heels, studied her so blatantly she felt her cheeks heat. "How was your day?"

"My day?" Acutely aware of the banality of their conversation, she nonetheless was grateful for his ability to ward off awkward silence. "It was fine, thanks."

"You're feeling better today, I see." Reacting to her shocked stare, he had the grace to look embarrassed. "I called the store yesterday to see if you and Bobby would like to have dinner with me after practice. They indicated you'd called in sick."

Chessa was so stunned she didn't know what to say. Finally she blurted out, "How did you know where I worked?"

"Bobby told me." Nick tilted his head, intensified his scrutiny. "Was it supposed to be a secret?"

Flushing madly now, Chessa feigned interest in a group of uniformed youngsters whispering together beside the bleachers. "I'm not ashamed of my job, if that's what you mean." In comparison to Nick's success, an accounting clerk in a discount department store seemed rather ordinary. "Not everyone is cut out to run his own business."

A subtle straightening of his shoulders was the only indicator that her reply had startled him. "Actually, you do run your own business, and a very creative one it is. I admire that."

Oddly deflated by the praise, she could muster only a thin "You do?"

To which he flashed another one of those killer smiles and issued a slow, sexy nod that practically buckled her knees. "I strongly support the entrepre-neurial spirit in all its myriad designs."

She managed a thin smile, feeling supremely fool-ish. "Most people would call what I do a cute little hobby."

"Hobbies don't have a national clientele, or the potential to expand into a full-fledged corporate en-deavor."

"Corporate—?" She blinked, felt the giggle roll off her tongue before she could stop it. Covering her mouth, she struggled for control and was grateful for the distraction of Bobby running back from the rest room, clutching the same department store bag.

He glanced around, spotted Nick over by the car, then slowed his advance and held the bag behind his back. Sidling over with a nervous twitch in his eye, he moved beside Nick while angling a glance at his mother. "We gotta go," he told her importantly. "Practice is starting."

"All right." Chessa leaned around, trying for a better look at the bag behind her son's back. "What's that?"

Bobby widened his eyes. "Nothing."

"May I see it?"

"It belongs to Dad," he said, then shoved the item against Nick's chest. "We gotta go."

Struggling against a smile, Nick took the bag with one hand, laid the other on Bobby's small shoulder. "You go on, son. I'll be right there."

After a moment's hesitation, Bobby trudged to-ward the field casting worried glances over his shoul-der.

As soon as he joined his teammates, Chessa whirled on Nick. "What was that all about?"

"What was what about?"

"That." She poked a finger in the direction of the bag he held at his side, and wasn't fooled by his innocent expression.

"This? Nothing important." As he raised the bag, a mischievous gleam lit his dark eyes. "Just man stuff."

"Man stuff? Oh, please." She snatched the bag, peered inside and nearly fainted. "An athletic supporter?"

"Actually it's a sports cup," he replied affably.

"I don't care what you call it, why did you bring it here?"

"Er, Bobby asked me to."

"I've already purchased all the equipment he needs, including a...a...sports cup." Furious, she shoved the bag into his hand. "He doesn't need this one."

"True." Grinning madly, Nick neatly closed the bag, seemed to be dreadfully amused by something. "This is the one you bought for him. It was too small."

"Too small?" Her jaw drooped so quickly she practically felt pavement burns. "They come in sizes?" When he hiked a brow, she prayed the ground would open and swallow her whole. Giving in to the urge to twist a hank of hair around her finger, she managed a casual shrug. "I was unaware of that. If Bobby had simply informed me the item was, er, improperly fitted, I would have rectified the situation."

Nick could barely contain his amusement. "I'm certain you would have, but he was embarrassed to tell you. You know how boys are."

Clearly her son hadn't been too embarrassed to tell a man he barely knew, which galled Chessa to the bone. "Of course I know how boys are." The reply was suitably frosty, although much of its impact was lost as her hair-tangled fingers became knotted against the side of her head in a twisted salute. She lifted her chin a notch higher, pretended to enjoy carrying on the conversation with a finger tied to her ear. "If you don't mind, I'd like to find a seat now."

To Nick's credit, he made no mention of Chessa's predicament, although the tremble of his shoulders bore mute testament to the effort of controlling himself. His mouth twitched, twisted, quirked up at the corners. He cleverly turned a chuckle into a cough. "I'll see you after practice then. For dinner."

She would have given anything to cast a withering look over her shoulder, but since that would have derooted a good portion of hair, she settled for rotating her upper torso with as much dignity as she could muster. "I don't recall agreeing to that."

"You didn't. Bobby did."

"When?"

"When I telephoned the house last night. Apparently you were working in the basement." Amusement softened into concern. "He didn't tell you?"

"No, he didn't."

"He probably just forgot. You know how—"

"Yes," Chessa ground out between tightly clamped teeth. "I know how boys are."

With that she marched toward the bleachers, sat beside a startled woman and roughly disentangled her hand, pulling enough hair along with it to make her eyes water.

On the field, the game began. For the next two

hours, Chessa watched with a sense of wonder. She'd seen lots of her son's soccer games, but this one was different. Something was happening down on the field, something precious and beautiful. Every time Bobby and Nick exchanged an excited high-five or a spontaneous hug or a look of unmistakable father-son pride, Chessa's heart felt as if it had been squeezed.

By the time the game was over, Chessa had made her decision. The happiness on her child's face showed her more eloquently than words how much he had needed a father. Now he had one. Even if it meant living a lie, Chessa couldn't take that away from him. Not now.

Not ever.

Chapter Four

The pizza parlor vibrated with hoots, howls and the happy laughter of uniformed soccer players celebrating the completion of their first official game. Video games blasted and blared. Younger children scampered to a play center complete with plastic slides, tubes and a pool of colorful balls into which the little ones could dive. Adults swiveled through the crowd ferrying steaming pizzas and sloshing sodas to ravenous youngsters.

A loss hadn't dampened team spirits. The Marysville Muddogs had played well, well enough for each teammate to earn at least one gold star of excellence to adorn a spiffy new windbreaker. Nick Purcell had provided the stars along with purple nylon jackets embroidered with the team logo. It had been an unexpected gift, one the boys clearly cherished. Despite the warmth of the crowded restaurant, not a single team member had removed his jacket.

At the center of the celebration, a throng of excited

boys clad in purple crushed like a cluster of happy grapes around a table where Nick Purcell explained the fine art of sugar-pack thumb wrestling. It was a peculiar ritual in which combatants hooked pinky fingers together while attempting to dislodge the emptied sweetener pack sheathing the opponent's thumb.

From her vantage point at a corner booth, Chessa watched in fascination as Bobby hovered beside his newly discovered father, puffing with pride. It had been barely two weeks since Nick Purcell had entered their lives, initiating the emergence of an anxious, wary youngster into a happy, outgoing child. The transformation had been nothing short of miraculous.

"The way they're celebrating, you'd think the team had actually won." Molly Johnson shifted her pregnant bulk and used a crumpled napkin to wipe her two-year-old's runny nose. She glanced up as a cheer echoed from the circle of pizza-chomping thumb wrestlers. "He's so great with kids. Not bad to look at, either. I can't believe you kept him a secret all these years."

Pretending she hadn't heard the comment over the din, Chessa sipped her soda without response. Molly had been her friend and confidante for years, a vivacious woman with a chilling instinct for discerning even the most carefully construed falsehood. Her own son called her a human lie detector, and Bobby had once been awestruck when his best friend's mom, in her dual role as his after-school day-care provider, had caught him embellishing his homework prowess without having cast so much as a glance at the work in question. Bobby thought her psychic, but Chessa suspected she was simply gifted at interpreting subtle shifts in body language. The dart of a tongue, the shift of a gaze, the restless tap of a finger or foot, all clues in Molly's relentless quest for truth.

Across the table she finished tidying up her toddler, then called across the room. "Danny, would you please take your sister over to the play area?"

A shaggy blond head popped up from the circle of youngsters crowded around Nick's table. "Aw, Mom, do I have to? We're having fun."

Weariness crept into the woman's eyes, a touch of indecision tempered by an indulgent smile. "All right, sweetie. This is your party, after all."

Shifting uncomfortably, Molly hauled the grunting toddler into that portion of her lap pregnancy hadn't usurped.

As she did so, Nick Purcell turned in his chair. His gaze skimmed Molly's struggle to quiet the restless child in her lap, then settled on Chessa with an intensity that made her blush.

The cacophony of sound instantly dissipated. Blood pounded past her ears, and her pulse oscillated into high gear. Just a glance, a smile, a smoldering look had the power to affect Chessa in ways she'd never experienced. Judging by the knowing glint in Nick's eyes, he was well aware of that.

Pivoting on the smooth wooden bench, she broke the visual stalemate, feigned interest in a youngster pounding the controls of a nearby video game. Unable to resist a final furtive glance, she diverted her gaze in time to see Nick whisper to Danny, who issued a cheerful nod, then loped over to scoop up his baby sister. "Nick said to bring Missy over to our table and give you a break."

"How nice of him." The woman flashed a grateful

smile, to which Nick responded by touching two fingers to his temple in a small salute that Chessa found incredibly sexy.

Apparently Molly did, too. "Oo-o-o," she hummed when Nick's attention had returned to the impromptu thumb tournament. "There are hunks and there are megahunks. How on earth did you ever let that one get away?"

Chessa's face felt as if it had been heated by a blowtorch. "Nice talk from an old married woman like yourself."

"Hey, don't be throwing the word *old* around. You'll be thirty yourself in a couple of years. Besides, I'm married, not blind. Face it, the guy's a fox." Molly chuckled, tightened a paisley scarf around a shaggy spout of untidy blond hair atop her head and cast a curious glance across the table. "That's hardly news to you, is it?"

Suddenly struck by an overwhelming need to pluck olive slices from a half-eaten slice of pizza, Chessa pretended not to notice her friend's skepticism.

Molly tapped the table. "Are you going to make me ask?"

"Ask what?"

"You know what." Heaving a sigh, Molly sipped her soda, then set the glass down with a thunk. "C'mon, give. I want details."

"I don't know what you mean," she murmured, feigning fascination with stacking olive rounds into a neat pyramid.

"So that's how you're going to play it, huh? Okay, fine with me." Molly leaned forward as if inspecting every blink, every nuance of Chessa's expression.

"We've known each other since the boys were in preschool, yet not once have you ever mentioned Bobby's father."

Pushing her plate away, Chessa managed a nonchalant shrug and forced herself to meet her friend's gaze. "It didn't matter." The moment the words left her mouth, she recognized her fib reflected in Molly's startled eyes. "I mean, it all happened so long ago."

Molly studied her a moment longer, lips pursed, head cocked in a thoughtful tilt that caused the untidy gush of hair to flop forward like a blond fountain. "Were you high-school sweethearts?"

The wooden bench was hard as stone, and suddenly just as cold. Chessa remained motionless. Squirming would have given her perceptive friend more of a clue than she was willing to offer. "Not exactly."

"Not exactly?" Molly skewered her with a look. "You mean, you weren't officially going steady?"

"No."

"But clearly you were—" Molly hiked a brow for emphasis "—very close."

The room was stifling. "Say, is it hot in here, or what? I can't understand why the boys won't take those jackets off."

Across the table Molly's astute gaze shifted from Chessa to Nick and back again. After a moment she chuckled under her breath. "Okay, I get it. Y'all are trying to be discreet. News flash, hon. It's not working. There isn't a soul in this restaurant who can't feel the heat between you two."

Clearly pleased with herself, Molly giggled and sipped her cola, batting her eyes at Chessa, who was totally flummoxed until she followed her friend's subtle nod to where Nick was staring with nuclear profundity. A jaunty tilt of his head, a sexy tousle of hair ruffled by wind and ineffectually finger combed into submission, a straight slash of brow shadowing eyes that at first glance seemed ordinary, but now gleamed with magnetic force. Mesmerized, Chessa could not look away, was drawn by the intensity of his gaze like a moth to the deadly, flickering flame that will eventually consume it.

The room dimmed into a tunnel of darkness surrounding a man so incredibly handsome that her breath clogged in her throat. Blood raced through her veins as if seeking escape. She heard nothing but the pounding of her own heart, saw nothing but the wanton luster of his eyes, the determined set of his mouth. In her mind, in her sight, only Nick remained illuminated, glowing with ethereal allure.

Time literally stood still. For the first time in her life, Chessa understood what that meant, and was blissfully unaware of whether hours had passed or mere seconds. Only when Nick suddenly pushed back his chair and stood was she jarred from her reverie.

She heard a startled gasp, realized that it had come from her. Before she could exhale, Nick loomed above her, a smile on his lips, sensual hunger smoldering in his eyes. "May I join you?"

Chessa panicked when her voice failed. Thankfully, Molly suffered no such malady. "I thought you'd never ask," she chirped, issuing a grin so broad her dimpled chin appeared to be momentarily detached. "Pumping Chessa for the juicy stuff is like trying suck milk out of a fence post."

"So, it's juicy stuff you're after." Chuckling softly, Nick slid onto the bench, pressing his arm against Chessa's shoulder. Her flesh quivered at the intimacy, but she made no effort to move away. She didn't know why. "Maybe I can help you out there. What do you want to know?"

If he felt her stiffen, he gave no outward indication beyond looping a lazy arm around Chessa's shoulder, which nearly startled her into a seizure. He tilted his head until his breath brushed her ear, and raised the fine hairs at her temple. "Relax, darling," he whispered loudly enough to be heard by the fascinated woman across the table. "We have no secrets from your friends."

"Right!" Molly blurted, unable to contain her glee. "No secrets from your friends. So tell me, were you high-school sweethearts, torn apart by families who couldn't understand young love? Were you tragically separated by the cruelty of circumstance? Have you pined for each other all these years, only to be reunited with a passion that never died, a desire that still throbs deep inside—"

Chessa found her voice with a vengeance. "Good grief, Molly! What *have* you been reading?"

A roar of laughter shook the manly chest against which Chessa found herself pressed. "True," Nick said amiably, squeezing her shoulder as if warning her to remain silent. "All true. We were high-school sweethearts, deeply in love, of course."

"Of course," Molly murmured, clearly captivated by his charm.

As was Chessa, who could only stare at Nick in utter disbelief. He smiled as if she were a goddess in a grass-stained sweatshirt, lifting one of her hands to his lips to brush a sensual kiss on her palm. Protest died on her tongue, pinned there by an exquisite shiver of sheer delight. The warmth of his mouth on her skin, the sensation of pleasure as he lightly nipped each fingertip, then rubbed a subtly stubbled cheek against delicate flesh of her inner wrist, bathing her with electric heat.

She was utterly speechless.

Molly wasn't. "It sounds so beautiful." She sighed. "But what happened, why didn't you stay together?"

"Hmm?" Nick's eyes clouded as if he'd completely forgotten about the excited woman across the table. The moment passed quickly, with a clarifying blink and a sophisticated shrug. "Unfortunately I was at an age where adventure beckoned, and I answered the call without realizing that what Chessa and I shared was very special."

The interrogation continued. "You didn't know Chessa was pregnant?"

"No." He actually flinched. "That's no excuse, of course. My behavior was selfish. I take full responsibility for it." When he gazed at Chessa again, there was sincerity in his smile, and an exquisite sadness that pierced her heart. "I didn't deserve Chessa then, and I don't deserve her now. My only hope is that she'll forgive the unforgivable and allow me to be a part of my son's life. And hers."

Across the table, Molly sniffed, snatched a napkin and made a production of dabbing her eyes. "That's the sweetest thing I've ever heard."

Fortunately there was no need to reply. Not that Chessa could have uttered a single word even if she'd wanted to. Only when the ache in her chest became unbearable did she realize she'd forgotten to breathe. Air rushed out like a sensual sigh, which Molly took as a request for privacy. Heaving her bulk awkwardly, the woman rose from the cramped booth, muttered something about checking on the children.

After Molly left, Nick made no move to remove his arm from Chessa's shoulders, or to release her hand. "You look lovely."

She looked like hell, and she knew it. After she'd screamed herself into a sweat at the soccer game, what little makeup she'd worn had dripped off hours ago and her hair was plastered to her scalp like mummified roadkill. Having been a mom for the past nine years, Chessa recognized a diversionary tactic when she saw one and called him on it. "Forget the sweet talk. We no longer have an audience."

An amused twitch hiked the corner of his mouth, but only for a moment. "The audience surrounds us."

Unable to dispute that dozens of curious eyes were watching, she managed what she hoped was a suitably outraged shrug. "That's beside the point."

"Is it?"

"Of course." Determined to maintain eye contact until he looked away, she was oddly deflated when he finally broke the visual stalemate with an expression of regret mingled with supreme sadness. She moistened her lips. "I hope you realize that whopper you just told Molly will be all over town by tomorrow morning."

"I'm counting on it."

"Why?"

"Because human nature being what it is, people are bound to speculate about me, about us, about our past relationship. I don't want them thinking of you as a loose woman, or pity Bobby as the issue of some sordid back-seat affair." Sucking a deep breath, Nick squeezed her hand, studied it as if searching for secrets. "What happened that night after the dance was my fault, Chessa, not yours. I was drunk, stupid, willing to trade a vulnerable young girl's future for my own pleasure. You've already suffered enough for my selfishness."

Now it was Chessa's turn to look away. Every drop of blood seemed to drain from her head. The room spun like a crazy top. Breath came in shallow gulps of guilt and remorse. She wanted to erase the pain in his eyes, to assure him that he'd done nothing wrong. At least, not with her. "Nick, please, it was a long time ago."

A ragged edge sharpened his voice. "Chessa?" Despite a determination not to, she looked at him, and nearly fainted at the desperation in his eyes. "Tell me I wasn't…unkind to you."

"Unkind?" For a moment she honestly didn't understand. When she realized what he meant, it nearly broke her heart. "No, Nick, I was never forced into anything I didn't want to do."

That much was true, at least. She couldn't bear the guilt in his eyes. Truth rose into her throat, nearly spilled out. "Nick, about that night—"

"I know, I know. I remember."

"You do?"

"Every moment." A subtle skitter in his gaze betrayed him. "Well, almost every moment. Parts of the evening are a little hazy." A boyish half smile tugged at her heartstrings. "That's one reason I don't drink anymore."

Although she'd vaguely noticed that Nick had ordered soda while most of the men shared pitchers of beer, she hadn't attached particular significance to it. "Er, how much do you actually remember about, umm, that night?"

His tongue darted out to moisten his lips. "The dance was nearly over. Kids were hanging out in the parking lot, all dressed in poodle skirts, bobby socks, ponytails, styles of the fifties. I was there with my friends. You were there with yours." A furtive glance posed a mute question to which Chessa could not reply. "I guess neither of us was ready for the evening to end."

A lump of pure misery settled in the pit of her stomach, partly at the bittersweet memories, partly at the irony of just how accurate Nick's description had been.

The fifties sock hop had been a tradition at her hometown high school, and Chessa had been there. The dance had been glorious, the highlight of her young life. She hadn't wanted it to end. She'd wanted moonlight and romance. She'd wanted passion and sweetness. She'd wanted love.

So Bobby had been conceived that night, just as Nick had presumed. There was, however, one inaccuracy in the details Nick had pieced together. A big one.

Tears gathered, blurring her vision. She shook her head, moaning. "This isn't right. All the lies, then more lies, then more lies to cover the lies. It just isn't right."

"Chessa, please." He slipped a thumb beneath her chin, urging her to look at him. "I know how you feel. I feel the same way. Finding you again, finding my son, is the most important thing that has ever happened to me. I never realized how much I was missing, how alone I truly was. There's no way I can ever repay the joy you and Bobby have given me." He paused to caress her cheek with his knuckles. "Sometimes a lie is necessary to protect a higher truth."

Torn, Chessa gazed at this man of honor, this man who was willing to publicly risk his own reputation in order to defend hers, who took such joy from giving of himself to a child who so desperately needed him.

Sometimes a lie is necessary to protect a higher truth.

The decision rolled off her tongue a moment before her heart embraced it. "Yes," she murmured. "Sometimes it is."

Cracking open the back door, Nick peeked into the kitchen, then whispered over his shoulder. "All clear."

Bobby scampered up the steps with his hands cupped to contain his captured prize. Peering under his dad's arm, he gave the deserted kitchen quick scrutiny before ducking inside.

Nick followed, easing the door closed behind them. He tiptoed over to peek into the living room. It, too, was deserted, except for the curious cat sitting on the odd-looking steamer-trunk table. Sensing a break in monotony, the animal hopped down and ambled into the kitchen to check out this interesting new activity.

Meanwhile Nick's gaze settled on the open door beneath the highest point of the stairway banister, and the soft spray of fluorescence spilling up from the work area below. "Your mom is in the basement," he whispered. "The coast is clear."

Bobby giggled, held his cupped hands up to peer beneath a slightly raised thumb. "This is gonna be so cool. Mom will freak."

Grinning, Nick moved toward a row of drawers in the lower cupboards, opening each to check its content. One contained a hodgepodge of spare batteries, a flashlight, opened envelopes that appeared to be bills awaiting payment and a couple of sprung mousetraps resting between calls to duty. Another drawer was filled with neatly folded kitchen towels, potholders and a couple of woven wicker trivets. The top drawer contained silverware and other kitchen utensils. "How about this?"

Bobby scampered over, pursed his lips. "Nah. Too many sharp knives. He might hurt himself."

"Right." Nick closed the drawer, turned his gaze on the upper cupboards that held canned goods and other foodstuffs. "Nope, not here." Mugsy the cat hopped onto the counter to watch Nick inspect a cupboard of mixing bowls and casserole dishes. "How about this?"

"Mom doesn't use that stuff everyday. He could starve before she found him."

"Good point." The next cupboard held plastic tumblers, bowls and dinnerware. "Surely these items would be used frequently."

"Aw'right!" Clearly excited, Bobby dashed over and allowed Nick to lift him up until his upper body was parallel to the open cupboard. "Okay, Sidney," he whispered against his cupped hands. "Do your thing."

With that instruction, the boy carefully opened his hands, allowing a six-inch skink to scamper across the stacked dinner plates, and settle into a nest of plastic cereal bowls. The lizard performed a series of impromptu pushups, peering over the edge of the bowl with each lift as if requesting praise for his prowess.

Bobby was clearly elated. "Too cool!" he exclaimed as Nick lowered him to the floor and closed the cupboard. "Mom's gonna choke when she sees him. It'll be so funny."

"One hopes." Nick was already having second thoughts. "Your mom does have a sense of humor about such things, right?"

"Sure she does." An indecisive pucker furrowed across his forehead. "I mean, she laughs at cartoons and stuff."

"And you're sure she's not frightened of lizards?"

"Nah, she thinks they're cute. She rescued a real fat lizard from Mugsy once. It had a scratch on its back, so she put antiseptic on it, and kept it in a little box until it was all better."

Nick rubbed his hands together and grinned. He'd always loved practical jokes, much to the dismay of his office staff, most of whom rarely lifted a brow when noting a rubber fly floating in the coffeepot or a fake spiderweb arranged in an often-used file cabinet. No harm was ever done. Nick figured his staff could use a chuckle now and again. Laughter was good for the soul, after all. Nick only teased people he liked.

He really liked Chessa.

With a wink and a grin, Nick ruffled his son's hair.

"I'm getting kind of hungry, sport. How about you?"

Recognizing the clue, Bobby broke into a fit of giggles. He dashed into the living room, skidded to the open door and hollered down into the basement. "Mom, can we have lunch now?"

Nick moved into position behind his son, listening for the reply. It came quickly.

"It's not even noon yet," Chessa called back.

"But we're real hungry."

"A couple of cookies should hold you for a while."

"No, no, we don't want cookies. We're hungry for, umm…"

Bobby shot a questioning look at Nick, who shrugged helplessly. The image of Sidney the lizard doing pushups in a nest of bowls flashed into his mind. "Soup," he whispered.

"I don't like soup," Bobby whispered back.

"Bowls, Bobby, bowls."

"Oh, yeah." Grinning, the boy hollered, "Soup! We want soup."

"You don't like soup."

"I do now."

A sigh of frustration filtered up the stairs. "I thought you and Nick were practicing for the father-son picnic."

"We were. We can do the three-legged race in four minutes now, and I can catch an egg from thirty feet away without breaking it, and we can do spoon runs, and the hot-dog relay, and…and…" A desperate glance brought in reinforcements.

"That's why we're so hungry," Nick added

loudly. "But if you're busy, we can make our own lunch."

The suggestion was met by a startled clunk and frantic shuffling sounds. "Don't you dare mess up my clean kitchen. I'll be right there."

Spinning around, the grinning child exchanged a high-five with his chuckling dad, then headed back to the kitchen for a finale that turned out to be far more exciting than either could have anticipated.

Chapter Five

"Quit wiggling."

"It hurts."

"Good." Pinning Nick's wrist against the kitchen table, Chessa dabbed a cotton ball dipped in stinging antiseptic on angry scratches along his forearm. "Serves you right for trying to scare the wits out of me."

"We weren't trying to scare you." Sulking adorably, he shifted in the chair, eyeing his wounds with the same forced courage her son used in similar circumstances. "We thought you'd be amused."

"Amused, is it?" She peevishly soaked another cotton ball with iodine, held it in front of his startled face like a drippy orange threat. "Exactly what, pray tell, did you think I'd find amusing about wearing a lizard in my hair?"

"Who knew it could jump that far?"

"The cat knew."

He flinched, ducked his gaze to the annoyed feline

perched on the edge of the table. "Traitor." The animal narrowed its eyes, thwacked its tail in agitation. "I should throw you to that snarling rottweiler down the street."

Mugsy hissed. Chessa chuckled.

Nick sighed. "The dog wouldn't have a chance, would he?"

"Not a one," she replied cheerfully, grasping a well-muscled arm to inspect the remaining war wounds. "At least Mugsy tried to protect me. He will, of course, be amply rewarded."

"That vicious beast shredded my arms, tried to claw my eyes out and damn near had himself a lizard lunch. I'd say that was reward enough."

"Not quite. *This* is reward enough." She pressed the iodine-soaked cotton on a nasty gouge beneath his elbow. Nick howled, cut loose a string of angry epithets. "Naughty language, Mr. Purcell. Tsk-tsk."

Nick spun in his chair, skewered her with a look. "You're enjoying this, aren't you?"

"Oh, yes."

Looking mightily grieved, he yanked his arm away, studied the orange streaks dripping down his elbow, then angled a glance twinkling with the hint of a smile. "It was worth any amount of pain to see the look on your face when you opened that cupboard."

"I live to amuse."

"Couldn't you have just screamed a little?"

"Screamed? As in poor, terrified female goes into hysterics at the sight of a harmless river skink?"

"Something like that." He shrugged, flashing a dizzying grin. "Your stoic courage cost me five bucks."

It took a moment for that to sink in. "You bet on
what my reaction would be?"

"Uh-huh."

"You actually placed a bet with *my son?*"

"Our son." His grin faded. "It wasn't as if I expected you to faint. I just figured you'd at least, well,
squeak or something."

"Squeak. How flattering." She flung down the
used cotton ball, snatched up a new one. "Teaching
a nine-year-old to pull tricks on his mother and gam-
ble on the outcome. What a marvelous role model.
You should be so proud."

As she reached for the iodine bottle, Nick touched
her wrist. Her skin tingled beneath his fingers, a
warm vibration that enveloped her entire body in the
blink of an eye.

"You're right, of course. I wasn't thinking. I'm
sorry."

She licked her lips, fought a shiver of sensation as
she eased her hand away.

"I want to be a good father to Bobby," he said
quietly.

Her gaze skittered. "I know you do."

"I'll need your help."

"My help?"

"The prank was a mistake, and I'm sorry. I'll need
your help to keep from making more mistakes."

"It wasn't a mistake, exactly." Uncomfortable
now, she shifted from one side of his chair to the
other, feeling supremely guilty. "I mean, it was just
a joke. Children need to laugh as much as adults do.
Perhaps even more."

He regarded her, smiling. "It was funny, wasn't
it?"

Although Chessa's mouth twitched in response, she wasn't ready to let Nick off the hook quite yet. "I suppose that depends on one's vantage point. The lizard wasn't amused."

Nick's smile flattened as he glared at the fat cat seated across the table. "And whose fault was that?" Mugsy yawned hugely, as if he couldn't be bothered by a mere human's opinion.

"Don't go blaming the cat."

"My blood is on his claws."

"Your blood would be on my claws if Mugsy hadn't gotten there first." The threat was softened by a chuckle. Despite her attempt at indignation, she took some responsibility for the episode, and realized in retrospect that she should have guessed something was amiss when she'd entered the kitchen to find both Nick and Bobby sitting at the kitchen table, grinning madly and looking supremely pleased with themselves. If she hadn't been preoccupied, she might even have taken a cue from the twitching cat perched on the counter, staring at the cupboard as if anticipating a momentous occasion.

Certainly that's exactly what the two gloating delinquents at the table had expected. What they hadn't expected, however, was the chaos that followed.

The lizard shot from the cupboard like a reptilian bullet. The cat pounced. Both animals had simultaneously landed on Chessa's head, scrambled down her shoulders and hit the floor running. Bobby leaped up, hollering. Nick bellowed once, then hurdled the table with athletic aplomb that would have been admirable under other circumstances. The child dived for the scampering lizard. The man dived for the cat.

What followed had not been pretty.

Now cat and man glared at each other with mutual disdain.

"Bloodthirsty beast." Mugsy hissed, swatted at the accusing finger pointed in his direction. Nick yanked his hand back. "You see? The animal is a menace. It hates me."

"He's still upset that you grabbed his tail. Cats are notoriously testy about that."

"Well, I couldn't let him eat Bobby's lizard." One brow rose with a petulant arch. "Some people actually appreciate a man who suffers grievous injury to save a life."

Chessa laughed. "So you fancy yourself a hero?"

"Of course not." A twinkle, a twitch of a smile. "But I imagine the lizard does." Shifting his gaze, Nick batted a clean cotton ball with his fingertip. "Presuming, of course, said lizard doesn't dwell upon the details of how it got into the cupboard in the first place."

"Ah, yes, those pesky details. Turn your head. No, that way." A peculiar buzz vibrated her chest when she touched his chin to guide him. Her mouth went dry. She took a calming breath, while he tilted his head to expose a crisscross of tiny scratches along his jaw and cheekbone.

It was, she noticed, quite a handsome jaw. Sharp, well contoured, with just enough angle to be geometrically appealing, but not harshly so. His skin was soft, quite smooth, freshly shaven within the past few hours. A scent clung to him, clean and snappy, the subtle ocean tang of cologne.

"You're not going to put that stuff on my face, are you? I'll look like a geek at the picnic tomorrow."

"It'll wash off. Besides, my mother swears by iodine. Says it's the only thing strong enough to kill
all the germs."

"Your mother must be a sadist."

"As a matter of fact, she is. Stop squirming." She
steadied his head, allowing her fingertips to slip into
his hair. Soft hair. Thick, glossy, with a hint of
golden highlights buried in the soft sheen. She caressed him without conscious thought until she noticed an odd warmth in his eyes and the silent question. They were close. So close. His lips parted
softly, an invitation she desperately wanted to accept.

She wanted him.

The realization stunned her to the core. She actually wanted this man, wanted to taste him, touch him,
take him inside her. There was an aura of sheer sex-
uality about him, an aura so powerful it tugged her
from the inside out.

He touched her jaw, slid his thumb just beneath
her quivering lower lip. "Your chin is orange."

"Is it?" Breathless. She sounded positively
breathless.

"We match," he whispered, slipping his hand
around to cup the back of her neck.

"Yes, I guess we do." She shivered, tangling her
fingers in his hair while her free hand splayed against
his chest. Muscles tightened beneath her touch, the
subtle ripple of male flesh that made her palms itch
for more. It had been so long, so very long. Just a
kiss, one small, insignificant kiss. What would be the
harm? A touch, a taste, to sate her curiosity, soothe
the savage ache in her soul.

His palm caressed her nape, sending shivers down
her spine and setting every nerve in her body afire.

Lusty flames exploded deep inside, igniting secret places that hadn't been warmed in years. The loneliness, the need, the silent yearning that she'd not dared to acknowledge, all of the passion and promise she'd denied herself for nearly a decade erupted in her heart and in his eyes.

A kiss wouldn't be enough. She wanted all of him. Right now. Right there.

He knew it.

While his heart raced beneath her palm, his lips parted as he urged her closer. A puff of breath warmed her cheek. The scent of him excited her beyond measure. She closed her eyes, prayed that he would take her in his arms, pull her into his lap before her knees buckled. As if in answer to her silent call, his free arm encircled her waist at the same moment his lips brushed the corner of her mouth. The thrill took her breath away.

Just as she allowed herself to slip bonelessly into his embrace, the back door slammed open. "Mom, Dad! I took Sidney home and he ran right into a big clump of grass and— Hey, what are you doing?"

Chessa leaped up, frantically smoothing her clothes. "Nothing, sweetie, nothing at all." She fingered her mussed hair, managed a bright smile that did little to cool her burning cheeks. "We're, ah—" She tensed as she heard Nick's chair scrape away from the table, was acutely aware of him as he rose to stand behind her.

"Just a bit of first aid." He held out his orange-streaked arms. "Your mother is quite a talented nurse."

"Yeah, I know." Bobby frowned. "Gee, how come you used iodine, Mom?"

Nick stiffened. "Doesn't she use iodine on your scratches?"

"Heck, no! That stuff stings."

With that pronouncement, the youngster went to retrieve a soda from the fridge. Nick leaned over, whispered against Chessa's ear. "You realize, of course, this means war."

She smiled. "Of course."

"Miss Needer, Miss Needer!" Nearly tripping on a rise in the grass-covered hill, Bobby flailed his way toward a smiling middle-aged woman surrounded by giggling youngsters. "This is my dad, Miss Needer, my real dad!"

The woman cocked her head, regarded Nick with friendly curiosity. When Nick trudged within reach, she extended a hand. "Welcome to our father-son picnic, Mr. Purcell. Bobby speaks of you so often I feel as if we've already met." Her gaze dropped to the slime dripping down the front of his fashionable golf shirt, remnants of an egg-toss misstep that had cost them the first-place ribbon. Nick had been disappointed, but Bobby didn't seem to care. The youngster proudly clutched his red ribbon along with the first-place blue they'd garnered for the three-legged race and several honorable mentions for competitions in which they'd failed to place.

More embarrassed by the fuss his son was making than by the mess oozing down his shirt, Nick accepted the woman's hand gently, was surprised by the firmness of her grasp. "I've heard a great deal about you, as well, Miss Needer. Bobby considers you to be the finest teacher on the face of the earth."

"Does he?" She smiled at the boy with such af-

fection that Nick liked her instantly. "He's a wonderful student. You must be very proud." The
teacher's gaze slipped beyond Nick's shoulder.
"Chessa! Such a wonderful day for a picnic. Isn't it
lovely that Bobby's father was able to participate this
year?"

"Yes, lovely." Although responding to Miss
Needer, Chessa's rapt gaze was focused on her son.
The youngster was beaming, his cheeks flushed with
excitement, gleaming with perspiration and framed
by a tousle of fun-dampened hair. She gazed at the
child with a look of wonder and delight, as if nearly
moved to tears by the sheer magnitude of her son's
joy. "Bobby is having a wonderful time," she said.

"We both are," Nick countered. She blinked up
at him, eyes softened with poignancy, and what could
have been gratitude. Whatever it was, it touched him.

"I know." It was a whisper, almost a breath, that
spoke volumes. Simple words with a symbolism and
significance he knew was there but couldn't quite
identify.

Nick understood that something profound was
happening. He saw it in her eyes, felt it burst and
spread deep inside him. A sweet ache. A healing
need. A loosening of barriers that had been in place
so long he'd never noticed them.

He wanted to dwell on that, digest it, concentrate
on the plethora of peculiar sensations radiating
around a heart that was suddenly tender, exquisitely
raw. There was no chance for introspection as Bobby
leaped forward, snagging his belt buckle to spin him
around.

"Scotty!" the child hollered, hauling his bewildered father toward a gangly youngster in a grass-stained jersey. "Look, Scotty, look! This is my dad, my real dad!"

The boy named Scotty responded with a blank stare, although a man beside him, presumably his own father, acknowledged the introduction with a friendly wave. Before Nick could return the gesture, he was again whipped around by the belt, dragged toward yet another group of laughing youngsters and puffing, sweat-drenched men. "Chad, Jamie, this is my dad! Joey, look, here's my dad, my real dad!"

One of the men angled an empathetic glance at Nick's slimy shirt. "Egg toss, eh? Yep, that's a tough one." He nodded toward a similar stain on the thigh of his own khaki pants. "Spoon race is the worst, though. It's enough to stop a man's heart on the spot. You two entered in all the events?"

Nick sighed. "It certainly feels like it."

A forceful yank, and he found himself stumbling toward yet another mulling group while his son hollered the now-familiar mantra. "Look, guys, this is my dad, my real dad!"

From the corner of his eye Nick glimpsed Chessa turning away and moving toward the burgundy plaid blanket where their picnic lunch awaited them. She seated herself, staring into space as if so immersed in thought as to be unaware of her surroundings. She seemed so distant, so fragile. So alone. A lump rose in Nick's throat, along with an overwhelming desire to be with her, to touch her hand, gaze into clear blue eyes and bask in the warmth of her smile.

Without taking his eyes off the woman, he laid an instinctive hand on the child. "I'm getting hungry. How about you?"

"Nah, not really. Ooh! There's Annie and Marsha! They're in my class. C'mon, Dad."

"Later, Son, after lunch."

"But I want them to see you." Bobby whirled, grabbed the hand from his shoulder with an imploring tug. "Please?" Nick was just about to refuse again when a sudden surge of moisture gathered in the boy's eyes. "Don't you like being my dad?"

A cannon shot to the chest couldn't have shaken Nick more. He stood there, stunned by the sheen of tears glimmering against his son's lashes, tears that he had caused.

An image from the past enveloped him, more vivid than a dream, more painful than reality. He saw his mother's face, pale but beautiful, her sculpted cheeks sunken with illness he'd been too young to recognize. Nick remembered how she'd smiled at him, softly, sweetly, with the same maternal love shining in Chessa's eyes when she gazed upon the face of her own son.

Voices echoed in his mind, memories of a time that had been both joyous and painful, a time when he'd known his own mother's unconditional love. "Of course your father loves you," she'd crooned, wiping away his childish tears. "It isn't his way to show it, but never forget that you are his blood."

"I don't wanna be his blood," Nick had wailed. "He hates me, and I hate him, too."

"Never say that." The edge in her voice had stiffened him. Mama rarely spoke harshly. When she did, Nick listened. "Your father is a good man, Nicholas, but even good men have weakness."

"He's a drunk, Mama. People laugh at him, and they laugh at me, too."

"Alcohol is his demon. You are his strength. Love for you gives him courage to fight his demons even when his hands tremble and the sweat of need gathers at his brow. Not a drop of liquor has touched his lips this week, not one drop."

Nick hadn't been impressed. "He always promises to stop, Mama, but he never does."

"It isn't easy for him. What's important is that despite the pain, despite his suffering, he continues to try. Do you know why?" When he acknowledged he didn't, his mother had gathered him in her arms. "Out of love for you, because he understands that every boy needs a father to be proud of."

Even as the vision faded, Nick could still feel the warmth of his mother's embrace, could still smell the jasmine scent of her hair, the rain-washed freshness of her soft skin. He could still feel her sweet kiss on his brow, hear the husky tremor of a voice so gentle and loving that even the memory of it gave him chills.

Every boy needs a father to be proud of.

"Dad?" A sharp tug shattered the final vestige of memory, pulling Nick back from his painful past.

Bobby's desperate little face peered up at him. "I told Annie and Marsha all about you, and they said I was making it all up." The child threw himself forward, clinging to him with a desperation that pierced Nick's heart. "Please, Dad, I have to show them that you're real, I have to."

Fighting a sudden rush of emotion so volatile it shook him to the marrow, Nick hugged his son fiercely, then thumbed a streak of moisture from his grimy little face. "Well then, I guess we'd better go show them just how real I am."

The joy in Bobby's face was utterly transforming. Nick took his son's hand for a stately stroll through the crowd of happy parents and children.

Every boy needs a father to be proud of.

Every boy.

Shifting the sleeping child in his arms, Nick waited for Chessa to illuminate the darkened house, then quietly followed her upstairs. Bobby groaned softly as Nick laid him on the bed, then immediately drifted into a sound sleep, not even twitching as his mother removed his shoes and socks.

She pulled a pair of small pajamas out from under the pillow, little white pj's covered with space ships and cartoon characters. Nick smiled. He'd never owned such snazzy pajamas as a child. In fact, he couldn't recall owning any pajamas at all. Rather, he'd slept in his underwear and a large, torn T-shirt handed down from his father.

It had suited him well enough, since he hadn't known at the time that other kids slept in fleecy flannels studded with cool cartoons. He was glad his son possessed such pajamas.

His son possessed something even more valuable, something priceless beyond measure: a mother's love. Nick, too, had been given that priceless gift, and he cherished every moment, every memory of the woman who had caressed his hair just as Chessa now caressed Bobby's.

Fascinated, Nick watched this incredible woman smooth her son's tousled mop, then glide her soft fingertips delicately across his brow, down his cheek, along chin and jaw as if memorizing every nuance of her child's beloved face. A mother's love, the most precious gift in the universe. His son was truly blessed.

Just as Nick had been truly blessed.

A sudden sting behind his eyes turned him away. He felt like an intruder, a voyeur to this loving interaction of a mother with her sleeping child. Heaviness settled into his chest, wedged in his throat. Emotion, he realized, and was surprised by its strength. Backing away quietly, Nick went downstairs and waited.

Moments later Chessa joined him. Her eyes were moist, her smile serene. "This has been the happiest day of his life," she said quietly. "Thank you."

Nick could barely remember what his life had been like before Chessa and Bobby were a part of it. "It's been the happiest day of my life, too. I'm the one who should be thanking you." Reaching out, he lifted her hand, cherished its subtle softness between his palms. "And I do thank you, Chessa. I thank you for our beautiful son, and for being the wonderful woman that you are."

A flicker of appreciation warmed her eyes, then heated into something more intimate. A quiet passion, mingled with curiosity and a touch of awe. "You are the best thing that has ever happened to my son."

"No, you are." He raised her hand to his lips, was thrilled by her subtle shiver as he placed a tender kiss in the center of her palm. "You are his strength, his hope, his joy and his solace. You are his mother. You are his life."

For a moment Chessa gazed up in wonder, so still that Nick was afraid she'd stopped breathing. Then her chest shuddered, and a flash of white appeared as her teeth scraped her lower lip. She searched his eyes as if seeing something profound, something she'd never seen before.

All the wasted years, Nick thought, all the joys they could have shared, all the challenges they could have faced together, should have faced together. She'd faced them all alone. The heartache, the sorrows, the worry, all alone. Because he hadn't been there for her.

Guilt pinched him, a painful reminder. He stepped back suddenly enough to startle her, released her hand to retrieve a folded envelope from his pants pocket. "I'm sorry, I meant to give this to you earlier."

A tiny frown drew her brows together as she accepted the envelope. "What is it?" When he responded with an embarrassed shrug, she opened it, blanched to the color of pale sand.

His breath caught at her horrified expression. "I know it's not enough. There will be more as soon as I can liquefy some long-term investments and—"

"No." She slapped the check against his palm with enough force to move him back a step. "I don't need your money."

Bewildered, he watched the caution creep back into her eyes and stress lines reassert themselves at the corners of her mouth. "You don't have to need it, Chessa. Bobby is my son, and I'm financially responsible for him. I know this isn't enough for the past nine years, of course, and I've already begun the process of establishing monthly support payments that will—"

"No!" The word caught in her throat, pinned there with a gasp. She shook her head violently, cov-

ered her mouth as she turned away. "I don't need
your money, I don't want your money, and I won't
accept it. Please, don't ever mention this again."

Totally taken aback, Nick extended a hand. "It's
my responsibility, Chessa—"

A blood-curdling scream suddenly spun Nick
around, chilling him to the bone.

"Mom, Mom, where are you, Mom? *Mom!*"

Before Nick could will his feet to move, Chessa
ran to the base of the stairs and called out. "I'm right
here, sweetheart, Mommy is right here."

Then he gave a childish whine, no longer expressing the terrifying fear that had sharpened his initial
cry. "Mom?"

"Yes, Bobby, I'm here. Everything is okay. You
can go back to sleep now."

"Oh, okay." The boy's tone was completely normal now, much to Nick's shock. "G'night, Mom."

"Goodnight, sweetheart."

It was over as quickly as it had begun. Nick found
his voice. "What on earth was that about?"

Chessa took a deep breath, faced him warily. "I'm
not sure. It started when he was about five, shortly
after the death of a playmate's father."

"Night terrors?"

"No, not specifically. It's more closely associated
with sleep walking, because he's had somnambulistic
episodes, as well. Several times a week Bobby calls
out for me in his sleep. As soon as he hears my voice,
he's fine."

Nick recalled the first time he'd tucked Bobby into
bed, when the child had begged him to leave the hall
light on. "What does Bobby think causes these, er,
episodes?"

"He never remembers them." She moistened her lips, focused on him with shuttered eyes. "Thank you again for a lovely day."

"Chessa, perhaps we should discuss—"

"It's late, Nick." She turned away from him then, but not before he saw the faint flicker of regret as she opened the front door for him.

He had little choice but to step through it. "Of course. Another time." He paused on the porch. "Good night, Chessa."

"Good night, Nick."

Chessa saw his hesitation, noted the determined warmth in his eyes a moment before he slipped an arm around her waist and pulled her against his chest. His strength startled her, awed her, yet she wasn't frightened of it, or of him. Heat radiated from the mountain of muscle against which she was pinned, along with an electric energy pulsating from his body into hers.

She knew he was going to kiss her. She knew, and she trembled with anticipation. It had been so long since a man had kissed her, so long since she'd wanted to be kissed. She wanted it now, wanted it with every fiber of her being.

A moment's pause gave him time to search her eyes, perhaps seeking silent permission. She gave it, lifting her lips, parting them more out of instinct than experience. His arm flexed, tightened, pressing her breasts against his chest. A tremor ran through him, through her, tingling her nipples into erotic knots.

A dip of his head, and his mouth took hers with more power than she'd dreamed possible. Moist, demanding, virile, the kiss shook her to the marrow, flooding her senses with an overload of emotion be-

yond her wildest dreams. This was not the tentative
peck of a child, not the sloppy smooch of a rushed
adolescent. This was a man's kiss, deep and probing,
with the unhurried, take-charge eloquence of one ac-
customed to decisive action. So profound was the
experience, so utterly compelling, that Chessa came
undone. Her toes curled, her knees buckled, and she
would have collapsed had he not been holding her
upright.

When Nick finally broke the kiss, both were
breathing hard and shaken to their soles.

He recovered first, a tremor in his voice the only
evidence that he, too, had been affected. "That was
even sweeter than I remembered."

Every drop of moisture evaporated from Chessa's
mouth. She couldn't have replied if she'd wanted to.
Fortunately she didn't have to. Nick brushed a thumb
over her brow, whispered good night, then strode
down the walkway to the curb where his car was
parked.

A moment later Nick's vehicle roared to life and
disappeared down the street. Only then did Chessa
close the front door and lean against the jamb, trembling. *Even sweeter than he remembered.*

Guilt enveloped her like a shroud. Nick was living
a lie. They all were, and yet she had no choice but
to perpetuate the charade for Bobby's sake, for her
parents' sake, and in a very real way, for Nick's sake,
as well. To purge her own soul meant destroying
everyone she cared about.

Confusion circled her like a sworn enemy, one she
couldn't understand and was helpless to defeat. How

could a lie that brought so much happiness be wrong, when the truth would bring misery to so many?

Living a lie came with a price. Chessa understood that, but she never could have imagined how high that price would be.

Chapter Six

It was a clear autumn morning, crisp and cool, with puffy clouds framing distant Sierra peaks and a sky as blue as his beloved son's eyes. Those eyes gleamed now, gazing up at him with a reverence that jostled Nick's heart.

As they strolled the dusty levee road, Bobby scooped up a flat rock to skim across the placid river. He flicked his wrist, and the pebble skipped over the murky water twice before disappearing into a circle of expanding ripples. "This is my favorite place in the whole word."

Palming another pebble, Nick eyed the serene wilderness beyond the man-made levee, a forest of buck brush and live oak studded with massive, lichen-stained boulders. "I can see why. It's beautiful." He deftly chucked his pebble, deliberately allowing only one skip so his son would not feel bested. "It reminds me of a place I used to go when I was about your age."

"Was it your secret place?"

"I suppose it was."

"I've got lots of secret places," Bobby said importantly. "Want to see one?"

"I'd love to."

Grinning, the boy scrambled down the levee slope, sloughing through knee-high snake grass without a hint of hesitation. Nick followed, wishing he'd worn something more appropriate to a wilderness hike than expensive worsted slacks and the pricy Italian loafers purchased in a moment of weakness, perhaps in small rebellion against the poverty of his youth. The foolishness of his footwear choice was even more obvious when he sank into a muddy boil bubbling at the base of the levee.

Cursing under his breath, Nick skimmed each side of the shoe on dried grass to remove the slimy goo, only to abandon the effort when he realized that he'd never liked the damned shoes, anyway. It was, he supposed, a fitting end to an extravagant symbol of overcompensation and arrogance. Shoes weren't important. People were important.

One of the most important people in Nick's life had just leaped onto an outcropping of granite bedrock, with the agility of a goat, and disappeared into a wall of weeping live oak. The youngster was fearless, Nick thought, a realization that both unnerved and pleased him. A brave child, who'd no doubt grow into a strong, courageous man.

Nick's heart swelled with pride. His child. His son. Flesh of his flesh, blood of his blood. Surely no father on earth had ever felt such incredible joy.

Swallowing a lump of surging emotion, he inhaled deeply, proceeded to squish his way to the boulder-strewn bedrock where he'd last seen his son. "Bobby?" Silence. "Where are you, Son?"

Heaving a sigh, he battled through a tangle of drooping branches into a roomy cave under the oak, carpeted by swirls of dried grass tamped into a nifty nest. Comfortable for a family of small animals or even a secretive child. Not so comfortable for a six-foot man bent like a human safety pin while twigs twisted in his hair and scraped the back of his neck as effectively as Mugsy's clever claws. "Bobby? The game is over. Where are you?"

Receiving no reply, Nick had little choice but to fight his way through the bush on the other side of the cozy cave, where he emerged in a forest of gnarled oaks, fragrant cedar, thorny blackberries and massive mounds of buck brush similar to the one through which he'd just passed. "Bobby?"

A hushed giggle drew his attention upward into the branches of a gnarled black oak. Leaves rustled. A thick branch jittered, and a familiar silhouette blocked a patch of sunlight, dappled as it passed through the fluttering fall foliage. "Come up here, Dad. You can see our house and my school and the soccer field and everything."

Nick had no intention of crawling up a tree like a hyperactive child. He was a grown-up, a mature adult, a businessman and a parent. It was his fatherly duty to explain that climbing trees was inappropriate, a dangerous activity that could result in serious injury. That's what Nick knew he should do, what he decided he would do. Just as soon as he was enjoyably settled beside the tree-clamoring child.

Grabbing a limb, Nick hoisted a mud-soaked shoe to brace his foot against the rough bark, and swung up into the canopy. A joyful whoop slipped from his throat, followed by delighted laughter he barely recognized as his own. For a brief, shining moment, Nick was a boy again, clambering through a childhood moment untainted by the unhappiness that had dogged so much of his youth.

By the time he settled onto the bouncing branch beside his giggling son, Nick's skin was scraped, his fancy worsted pants were torn, and his mature, adult spirit soared with a freedom he hadn't experienced in years. "You're right," he said, gazing out toward the buildings dotting the edge of town. "It's a great view."

Bobby was buzzing with excitement. "I told you!"

Nick looped an arm around the boy's shoulders, rubbed his palm over the slick purple satin of the Marysville Muddog windbreaker that had become Bobby's proudest possession. "Yes, you sure did."

They perched in the towering oak like a pair of happy scrub jays, admiring a vista of golden flatlands abutting forested foothills that melded into the snowy spine of the Sierras.

"Dad?"

"Yes, Son?"

"Did you climb trees when you were a kid?"

"Yes, I did, much to my mother's dismay." Nick smiled at the memory. "She was always afraid I'd break my neck."

"But you didn't."

"No, but that doesn't mean she wasn't right. Climbing trees is dangerous." The father in him burst forth without warning, surprising him. "You should never climb trees without supervision, Bobby.

If you were to hurt yourself, there wouldn't be anyone around to bring help.''

"I'm real careful."

"Accidents happen."

The boy shrugged, sent him a wary glance. "You're not going to tell Mom, are you?"

He should. He knew he should. "Not if you promise never to climb trees unless there's an adult close by."

"Aw-w." His small shoulders rolled forward. "Okay, okay, I promise."

It was a promise grudgingly given, one that would probably not be kept. Nick felt a twinge of regret at having elicited the pledge in the first place and couldn't quite identify what instinctive insistence of heart and mind had forced him to do so.

If he'd examined himself more closely, he might have recognized the fear, the exquisite, heartrending terror for the safety of this child he loved so dearly.

All of a sudden Bobby let out a squeak of revelation, as if he'd just realized something utterly momentous. "Your mom and dad are my grandparents, aren't they? I've got a whole 'nother grandma and grandpa! Do I have aunts and uncles, too? Danny's got lots of aunts and uncles, and a whole bunch of cousins, too. They play together all the time, and go to the beach and camping and stuff."

Alight with excitement, the boy bounced so abruptly that the branch gave a dangerous lurch. "How many cousins do I have? How many aunts and uncles? Where are my new grandma and grandpa? Can we go see them today? Please, please—?"

"Whoa, calm down or we'll both wind up in the

emergency room.'' Tightening his grip on his wriggling son, Nick wrapped his free arm around the tree trunk, hanging on for dear life until Bobby finally stopped fidgeting to gaze up with huge, hopeful eyes. Nick glanced away. "I don't have any brothers or sisters. There aren't any aunts, uncles or cousins.''

"Oh." His disappointment was palpable. He chewed his lip, swallowed hard and managed a brave shrug. "That's okay. When can we go see Gramma and Grampa?''

The realization that Bobby's curiosity about his paternal relatives was normal did little to ease Nick's pain at having to respond. He didn't want to talk about this, didn't want to explain his estrangement from the father who'd always disappointed him, or describe the exquisite loss of the mother he'd adored. "We can't go see them, Bobby."

"Why not?"

Puffing his cheeks, Nick blew out a breath. "Your grandma isn't with us any longer."

A blank stare confirmed that Bobby didn't understand the finality of that statement. "When is she coming back?''

"She's not coming back, Son. She passed away a long time ago."

A blink, a flicker of comprehension. "You mean she died?''

"Yes, Son. She died.''

Tears welled without warning, spilling down his face. "How come?''

"She was sick, Son, very sick.''

"Were you real little?''

"I was twelve.''

"I'm almost ten.'' His voice broke.

Nick read the fear in his eyes and answered it. "What happened to my mother is not going to happen to yours."

"How do you know?"

"Because your mother is strong and healthy."

"Jerry Morrison's dad died, too. He got in a car wreck."

Nick presumed young Jerry to be the playmate Chessa had referred to, the child whose tragic loss had affected Bobby so deeply. "Accidents sometimes happen, Son. That's why it's important for us to always be careful and not take unnecessary risks. We want to be around to spend time with the people we love."

A shiver ran from the boy's thin shoulders straight into Nick's heart. "That's what Mom says."

"Your mom is a very smart lady."

Bobby sniffed, wiped his wet face with the back of his hand. "I don't want you or Mom to go away. Promise you won't."

"We won't." Nick hugged him fiercely, so anxious to soothe the child's fear that he was willing to guarantee a destiny that was beyond control. "We won't ever go away."

That was exactly what Bobby wanted to hear. Clearly relieved, the child pivoted to straddle the branch. "Can we go see my grampa, Dad, can we, huh, can we?"

Nick's heart sank like a rock. "No, we can't."

"How come?"

The boy's crestfallen expression broke Nick's heart. "My father and I...we haven't seen each other in many years. I don't even know where he is."

Bobby's eyes snapped open as if spring loaded. "But we can find him. I found you."

"This is different." Nick paused to moisten his lips. "I don't believe he'd want to be found."

For a long moment, Bobby considered that. He frowned, fidgeted with a slender twig on which a trio of green acorns were forming. "My grandpa doesn't want me," he said finally. It wasn't a question.

"That's not true. He doesn't even know about you."

"How come?"

"Well, because I haven't told him."

"How come?"

"Because I don't know where he is."

"But we can find him."

Frustrated, Nick scoured his eyelids with his fingertips, unwilling to tell this trusting child that the grandfather he wanted so desperately to meet was probably passed out in a gutter somewhere, reeking of cheap wine. "This has nothing to do with you, Bobby. My father and I don't get along. It's sad, but that's the way things happen sometimes. We simply have to accept it and go on. Do you understand that?"

"Uh-huh." Eyes huge, Bobby stared up without speaking for what seemed an eternity, but was probably less than two minutes. When he finally spoke again, the power of his words nearly knocked Nick out of the tree. "Are you sorry you're my dad?"

"Am I—?" His throat closed, momentarily choking him. When he could speak again, his voice was raw, cracked like a shattered mirror. "You are the most wonderful son any man could have. Every day I thank God for you, and pray I can bring even a fraction of the happiness into your life that you have brought into mine.''

Tilting his head, Bobby regarded him somberly. ''So that means you like me?''

''I love you, Son. I will always love you.''

An impish grin burst free. ''Cool.''

Nick roared with laughter. ''Yes,'' he murmured, squeezing the youngster's satin-clad shoulders. ''It is pretty cool, isn't it?''

''Yep, pretty cool.'' Bobby giggled, squirmed, then gazed past Nick's head with a startled expression. ''Hey, Mom has company.''

Shifting, Nick followed the youngster's gaze and saw a familiar, white panel truck pull up in front of Chessa's house, which was about a mile away from their tree-top perch. ''They're here! Great!''

''Who's here?'' Bobby asked his father, who was already halfway down the tree.

''A surprise for your mom.'' Nick stepped onto solid ground, holding his arms up to assist the boy who was carefully picking his way downward.

Grinning like a fool, Nick could barely contain his glee. Pride had prevented Chessa from taking his money, but she was much too polite to refuse a gift, particularly a gift so perfect, so desperately needed. She would love it, absolutely love it.

Nick could hardly wait.

''No, I haven't told him, Mother.'' Clamping the receiver between her chin and shoulder, Chessa crossed the kitchen until the coiled phone-wire stretched to its full ten-foot length. ''Bobby and Nick adore each other. They couldn't be closer if they really were father and son. Bobby is happier than he's

ever been in his life. I can't take that away from him.
I won't—'' she dumped a measured pile of fresh apples into the sink, and turned on the faucet with more
force than necessary ''—and neither will you.'' The
forceful command and implied warning surprised
even Chessa, who rarely expressed dissent with her
parents' opinions, and under normal circumstances
wouldn't have dreamed of dispensing such a direc-
tive. These were not, however, normal circumstances. She'd painted herself into a corner of lies,
lies that if exposed would break her son's heart.
There was nothing she wouldn't do to protect Bobby,
to keep him happy and safe. Even if it meant chal-
lenging her own parents.

Other than sounding slightly stung, Marjorie made
no comment about the edict itself, or her daughter's
uncharacteristic mettle in having issued it. ''Of
course, dear. You already know where your father
and I stand on this matter.'' A sigh filtered through
the line, heavy with relief. When she spoke again,
however, her tone was wary, more restrained. ''But
do you really believe it's a good idea to allow Bobby
and, er, that man to spend so much time together?''

Chessa palmed the apple peeler, and stared out the
kitchen window toward the river levee, a half mile
away. They were out there somewhere, her cherished
son and Nick Purcell, a man of honor, empathy and
strong moral fiber, the absolute antithesis of the reck-
less, self-absorbed adolescent whose wild exploits
had once fascinated an entire town.

Perhaps the reputation had been ill deserved. Perhaps he'd simply grown up. Either way, Nick was a
good and decent man, who'd become father, mentor,

idol and friend to the son she loved more than life itself.

A passage from Bobby's letter flashed through her mind. *I don't want to borrow other people's dads any more....*

Now he didn't have to. As long as Chessa could protect her secret, Bobby would have his very own father to offer manly advice on manly things like sports protection devices, maintaining authoritative posture to avoid school bullies, even how to hide sweaty palms while talking to girls, topics Chessa hadn't dreamed would concern a little boy. "Nick Purcell has been the kind of father to Bobby that most kids can only dream of. He is kind and decent, honorable and strong, everything I want my son to emulate as he grows into a man. Nick means the world to Bobby."

And he meant the world to Chessa, although she wasn't prepared to admit that to her mother. Or even to herself.

"Of course, dear, of course. I simply thought that the more time they spent together, the more likely it would be that perhaps something might be noticed that could possibly, ah, cause questions to be asked."

Odd, Chessa thought, how conciliatory her mother sounded. She'd never noticed that weakness before, never been irritated by her nasal whine when wheedling something she wanted. It was a tone usually reserved for her husband, a submissive acquiescence tinged by apology for having the audacity to disagree or request that her own position be considered.

Compassion pushed annoyance aside. "I know, Mother. I've thought about that." Chessa had thought about little else these past weeks. "There's always the chance that something might happen to reveal that Bobby isn't Nick's biological child. There's a better chance that it won't. When you actually think about it, what proof does anyone have about who their parents are? How many families actually have DNA tests performed after the birth of every child? As for a lack of physical resemblance, that's hardly unique. After all, I look nothing like Daddy. He's tall and I'm short, he's blond and I'm brunette, he's lean as a willow whip and I have hips like the Queen Mary. When it comes right down to it, what proof do I have that we're even related?''

"Chessa!"

"You know what I mean, Mother." Frustrated, frightened, feeling slightly desperate, she whacked the peeler over the apple skin, futilely arguing with herself to rationalize the irrational. "There's more to being a father than an act of procreation. In every way that counts, Nick has been a father to Bobby, a good father, a real father. My son needs him." *I need him.* "My son wants him." *I want him.* "He's everything Bobby has ever longed for in a dad." *He's everything I've ever longed for in a man.* "I won't—"

She dropped the hacked-up apple in a lemon water bath, sagged against the counter, her throat constricted with emotion. The deception, the deceit, the frantic reasoning to justify a terrible lie. Was it really for her son? Or was some of it for her? "I won't let anything destroy that," she whispered.

For several long moments, the telephone was silent. When Marjorie finally spoke, her voice was gentle, filled with compassion and more strength than she'd expressed in a very long time. "It's all right, dear. I understand."

Exactly what she understood was left unspoken. That didn't matter. Chessa knew. Her mother knew. They both realized that Bobby wasn't the only one who was falling in love with Nick Purcell.

"Well." Marjorie cleared her throat, seemingly at a loss to say more.

Stunned by the emotional revelation, Chessa spun from the sink, automatically went to the pantry, her personal place of solace during moments of supreme stress or when life became too mystifying for comfort. She dragged the phone with her, searching her mind for a less volatile topic while she searched shelves for a soothing snack. "So, do you and Daddy want to come here for Thanksgiving this year?"

Her mother leaped upon the change of subject with audible relief. "I haven't thought about it, dear. It's nearly a month away."

"I know." Chessa rifled through a few boxes of unappealing crackers, sniffed a package of too-sweet cookies and finally settled on a tubular can of her favorite potato chips. "But you cooked last year, so I thought you might want a break—" She let out a shriek as a half-dozen cloth-covered springs shot from the can like a nest of exploding worms.

"Chessa?"

Heart pounding, she sagged against the pantry door, trying to breathe. She gasped, took one slow breath, then another. Last week she'd been jolted by the discovery of a rubber tarantula floating in the toilet. Yesterday she'd nearly had a heart attack when an incredibly realistic fake mouse poured out of the cereal box and plopped into her bowl.

Nick Purcell's influence, it seemed, was not completely without flaw.

"What is it, Chessa, what's wrong?"

"Nothing's wrong, Mother." Shifting the phone, she set the booby-trapped chip container on the counter. "My son has become quite the little prankster, that's all."

"Oh, my," Marjorie murmured. "That's so unlike him."

"Not anymore."

"How peculiar. He's always been such a shy, polite young man. I remember last year..." Marjorie's voice settled into a droning hum that slipped in one ear and out the other.

It wasn't that Chessa was being deliberately rude. Her attention had been captured by an odd sight outside the kitchen window. A strange truck was parked at the curb, a white panel van, similar to a small delivery vehicle. Three workmen stood in front of the passenger door, eyeing a clipboard and talking among themselves. One of them glanced at her house. Another nodded. All three moved toward the walkway, revealing a company logo stenciled on the passenger door: American Security Systems.

In less than a heartbeat Chessa realized she'd seen that logo on Nick's business cards. In the distance, two familiar figures loped along the levee road, one tall, virile and striking, one small, slender, clad in glowing purple.

"I have to go, Mother. I'll call you later." Chessa quickly hung up the phone, rushed to greet the trio of workmen on her porch.

The one with the clipboard tipped a worn work cap. "Here to install your new system, ma'am."

"New system?"

"Yes'm."

"There must be some mistake."

The man's smile flattened. He blinked rapidly, compared the house number to his clipboard, verified her name, then nervously wiped his brow with the back of his hand. "Got the order right here, ma'am. Top-of-the-line digital alarm with automatic feed direct to police and fire, instant-on panic mode, infrared motion sensors and—"

A co-worker elbowed him in the ribs, directed his attention toward the west side of the house. All three men snapped to attention as Nick Purcell jogged up, panting, disheveled, muddy and torn, as if he'd crawled through a bramble-filled swamp.

The man with the clipboard clicked his boot heels so smartly Chessa expected him to salute. "Mr. Purcell, sir."

Bobby swerved around Nick, skidded to the doorway, grinning madly. "Mom, Mom, isn't it cool? It's gonna be so great! I'm gonna show them exactly where I want mine!"

"Your—" she spun around as Bobby ducked under her arm and dashed upstairs "—what?" she finished lamely. Dropping her hand to her side, she cast a narrowed look over her shoulder.

"Trust me." Nick was grinning like a kid on Christmas morning. "You're going to love it."

"I love it!" Chessa ran a finger over the smooth control panel mounted in the wall at the landing of the basement stairs. Conveniently located within two steps of her worktable, the intercom system was a marvel of engineering, compact and discreet, with "speak" and "monitor" functions displayed by colorful lights mounted beneath a sleek ivory speaker. "It's perfect, absolutely perfect."

"I thought you'd like it."

"Oh, I do." She spun around, threw her arms around him. A quiver rippled through his body. His eyes darkened, a seductive heat that warmed her to the marrow. She gazed up, mesmerized. "Thank you," she whispered in a voice so vampish she barely recognized it as her own. "So much."

Nick swallowed hard, slid his palms along the ridge of her spine. "You're welcome."

He smelled so good, a tantalizing mix of earth and oak, of spicy tree bark and masculine desire. She had the overwhelming urge to lick his earlobe. She'd never wanted to lick an earlobe before, but she wanted to lick one now, wanted it with a vengeance, and she wouldn't have stopped there. Chessa craved the taste of him, all of him, every curve, every contour, every inch of sinewy muscle, every millimeter of masculine flesh.

So startling was both the urge and the intensity with which it struck that she stepped back, pivoted in the circle of his arms. His heat radiated against her back, weakened her knees. The memory of his kiss haunted her, the power of it, the profundity. The passion. She craved that passion, craved it so desperately it frightened her.

His palms splayed against her belly, pulling her against him until her bottom melded against his groin. She felt the quiver of his need, his hunger for her. A burst of sensuality nearly buckled her knees. Her belly boiled with yearning, knotted with a desire so fervent she was dizzied by the force of it.

Part of her feared he'd turn her around, crush her in his arms and kiss her senseless. Part of her hoped he would do just that, would scoop her into his arms and make mad, passionate love to her right there in the basement, between the bucket of wrinkled apple heads and the basket of dried wreath weeds.

Instead Nick suddenly loosened his embrace, slid one hand up to her shoulder, where it lingered without demand. A sharp intake of breath rattled his chest against her shoulder blades as he extended his free arm past her cheek and fingered the control panel. "From now on, all you have to do is keep the 'monitor' switch in the On position, the yellow light comes on, and you'll be able to hear Bobby when he wakes up. Then you just press the speak switch." He shuddered as she rubbed her cheek catlike against his forearm. "When the red light comes on, the receiver adds a 'send' signal, and you can speak to him without having to rush up the stairs."

"It's perfect," she murmured, tilting her head backward until her skull rested on his collar bone.

Air brushed her scalp as he exhaled all at once. "Bobby can use the control panel in his bedroom to call for you, and you'll be able to reply whether you're down here in the basement, in the kitchen, the garage, or even in the backyard."

"Umm-m." She couldn't stand it. Her heart was pounding, her pulse was racing, her legs felt like warm jelly. She sagged against him, sighing, and turned back in the circle of his arms. "I love the intercom system, Nick. It's wonderful." She tucked her head beneath his chin, snuggling against him as he caressed her hair. "But the alarm system seems unnecessary."

help if I can't fill them. I'm already working at max-
imum capacity.''

"You could handle it if you devoted all your time
to your business.''

"Quit my job?''

"Why not? You've created something very special, Chessa. You're bright, talented and have a sharp
business mind. You could turn Creations into a mil-
lion-dollar enterprise.''

"I could also go broke.''

He shrugged. "Not if you had another source of
income.''

Licking her lips, she deliberately disentangled
their fingers and forced herself to step away. "I'm
not taking your money, Nick. You know that.''

Disappointment clouded his eyes only briefly before he blinked it away. "Yes, I know that. I just
don't understand it.'' He studied her for a moment,
smiling as if he knew a delicious secret. "Would you
consider a partnership?''

It took a moment for that to sink in. "You want
to buy into my business?''

A dispirited downturn at the corners of his mouth
implied that wasn't exactly what he meant, but he
adjusted his expression quickly. "I'm always on the
lookout for sound investments.''

"Spoken like a true businessman.''

"That's what I am, as are you. The entrepreneurial
spirit is one of many things we share.'' He touched
her elbow, stopping her as she bent to gather an arm-
ful of mistletoe from the pile. "We have a lot in
common, Chessa. We'd make a good team.''

Searching his gaze, she recognized a deeper mean-
ing. She saw hope in his eyes, hope for a shared

future more intimate than his words had revealed. A sweet ache squeezed her heart, a turmoil of the soul she dared not acknowledge but could no longer ignore. The question burned in his gaze. She saw it, understood it, was helpless to respond.

After a moment he blinked, smiled, gave her shoulder a reassuring squeeze before focusing on the exuberant child gathering cattails across the dusty, rutted path by which adventurous vehicles accessed the bluff a hundred yards above them. "Bobby, your mom and I will be back in a few minutes."

The youngster spun around, clutching a bouquet of rangy wet reeds. "Where are you going?"

Ignoring Chessa's stunned stare, Nick replied with an offhanded shrug. "Just up the road a bit."

"Can I go, too?"

"Not this time, Son. We won't be long." Nick turned his face, but not before Chessa saw both his conspiratorial wink and her son's responsive grin. "So how about loading the cattails and mistletoe in the car trunk while we're gone?"

"You bet!" With a whoop of sheer delight, Bobby skipped happily over to dump his armload of wet reeds into the open trunk.

"Where are we going?" Chessa asked as Nick cupped her elbow to guide her up the narrow path.

"You'll see." He slipped his arm around her waist as if fearing she'd sprint and run.

Chessa had no intention of running. She could barely walk. His nearness, the heat of his body, the heady scent of dusty oak mingled with the fresh crispness of autumn air made her practically giddy. "This is a beautiful area," she murmured, struggling to change her focus from the sensual heat of his touch to the natural splendor of golden grasslands studded by stately oaks. "It was worth the drive. By the way, where are we?"

"Don't you know?" His quizzical glance should have cautioned her, but she was too filled with joy to notice that he seemed mystified by her question.

Filling her lungs, she tossed her head like a frisky mare, skipped ahead of him on the rocky dirt path. "All these foothill roads look pretty much the same to me, although I'll admit this area is one of the loveliest I've ever seen."

Nick frowned, but said nothing.

As they rounded a curve, the hill flattened into a barren plateau, crisscrossed with tire tracks, and marred by discarded bottles and beer cans. Beyond the clutter was a distant valley of verdant fields, isolated farmhouses surrounding a cluster of buildings that appeared to be a town. She rushed forward, clasping her hands in delight. "What a gorgeous view!"

Nick came up behind her. "It always has been."

There was a peculiar tension in his voice, a baffled quality that caught her attention. On edge now, she shifted, gazed back over the valley. A comment rolled off her tongue the same moment it entered her mind. "What a picturesque little village!"

She felt him stiffen, heard the sharp intake of breath. "That's Weaverton."

The stunning pronouncement jolted the smile off her face and shook her to her toes. This was it, she realized, the infamous lovers' lane, the passion pit that had evoked whispers in school corridors and giggles in the girls' locker room, the notorious view-point where windshields steamed and cars rocked with salacious passion, where virginity was lost and hearts were broken, where adolescent hormones were indulged and futures irrevocably altered.

And where an intoxicated young man had once found pleasure with a girl he couldn't remember.

Chessa swayed slightly, touched her throat. "It looks, ah, different in the daylight."

He regarded her. "Apparently you didn't come here often."

She licked her lips, shrugged, forced her gaze into the distance, now recognizing the familiar red building that housed the town's lumber store, and the steepled church just beyond the abandoned barn that she and her friends had used as a clubhouse. "I have never been here with anyone but you."

The answer was technically accurate, skillfully designed. It made her ill to realize how proficient she'd become at the art of evasion.

A smile slipped into Nick's eyes, a gleam of pride, of relief at believing that he'd been the only one with whom she'd shared this experience. "This is where it all began," he said. There was a touch of awe in his voice, a poignant wonder. "This is where our son was conceived."

Chessa stood immobile, unable to speak, barely able to breathe.

Moving behind her, he encircled her with his arms, clasped his hands below her breasts. "I wanted to stand here with you again, to return to this place so I could ask you...something." A sigh ruffled her hair, then he turned her around to gaze into her eyes with an intensity that made her shiver. "These past few weeks have been special. They've changed my life. You've changed my life." A perplexed frown lowered his brows. "What's this?" He touched her cheek, studied the moisture transferred to his thumb as if mystified by it. "Are you crying?"

"No," she said, although she clearly was. The burden of lies had broken her. She couldn't cope anymore, couldn't continue to deceive a man so dear that she'd have given her life to avoid hurting him.

Obviously baffled, he shifted his stance, struggled to speak. "Have I done something to upset you?"

She shook her head. "It's not you. It's me. I—"

"Mom, Dad!" A blur of motion caught her attention as Bobby dashed into the clearing, red-faced and panting.

Nick whirled, reached the frightened child in two strides. "What is it, son, what's wrong?"

"The car phone was ringing and ringing. I figured it might be important—" he paused to gulp a breath "—so I answered it. I was gonna take a message and stuff, just like you showed me. I didn't know— I didn't know..." Face twisted, Bobby extended his small grubby hands in a silent plea.

With Chessa beside him, Nick knelt down to the child's level and spoke in a soothing tone. "It's okay, Son, you did exactly the right thing. Tell me what happened."

"It was a lady. She told me to tell you—" A tiny sob caught in his throat.

"Tell me what, Bobby?"

"Grampa's real sick."

Chessa gasped. "Daddy? Oh, God—"

"No, Mom, my other grampa."

"Your other grampa?" Stunned, Chessa looked at

Nick, who rocked back to sit on his heels while the color drained from his face.

He never took his eyes off the distraught boy. "What exactly did the lady tell you, Bobby?"

"She said Grampa's in the hospital. She said we've gotta go there, Dad, we gotta go right now." Tears spurted from the child's eyes. "Please don't let my grampa die."

A hush of voices filtered from sterile halls, a whispered hum broken only by the occasional clank of a gurney, ring of a phone and the incessant electronic beep of the monitor mounted beside his father's bed.

Nick barely recognized the gaunt form beneath the sheets. Pale, with sunken cheeks and cracked lips, the man he'd once called Pop lay still as a corpse. Nick gazed at him, tried to muster the emotion a son was supposed to experience at such moments. There was nothing. Not love, not hate, not concern nor contempt. Just emptiness.

Despite that cruel denial issued so long ago, Nick knew this was his father, his flesh and blood, the man from whom his own life had evolved. There should be something, some ache of regret, some twinge of grief. There should be something.

The bedclothes vibrated, capturing Nick's attention. He straightened, moved from the foot of the bed to the side, where a metal tree held fluid-filled bags which hung like fat bats, dripping liquid into the maze of wires and tubes attached to the skeletal form beneath the covers.

One eye slitted open, then the other. Lou Purcell turned his head on his pillow, slowly, painfully, as if attempting to focus on something shadowy and elusive. Several seconds ticked by before his lips parted, and a weak voice emerged. "Hello, Son."

"Hello, Pop."

Lou blinked as if reassuring himself that the man beside his bed was indeed the person he thought. "Didn't think you'd come. Wouldn't have blamed you."

The ache surprised Nick, a nagging throb deep in his chest, filling the void with unexpected pain. "How are you feeling?"

"Bad."

It had been a stupid question. "The doctor tells me you'll recover."

"This time." Lou licked his lips, swallowed. "Need me a new liver."

Nick already knew that. "Transplants are routine nowadays."

Thin lips twisted into what could have been either a smile or a grimace. "Hell, ain't no one gonna waste a perfectly good liver on an old drunk."

That was true enough to make Nick flinch. "So stop drinking."

"Easier to stop living." Lou coughed, gasped, closed his eyes for a few seconds. "Got nothing to live for, anyway, since your mama died."

The ache in Nick's chest instantly exploded into an agony of sensation. He sucked a breath, steadied himself on the bed rail. Emotions poured like acid through his veins, bitter and biting, a surge of remembered anguish sweeping him back into the mind of that hurt, rejected child he'd once been. "You have me."

Nick couldn't believe he'd said that. If the shock in his eyes was any clue, neither could Lou.

A blink, a cloud, a shuttered look. Lou heaved a sigh that seemed to empty him out. "Never had you, Son. You always knew what I was. Yes, sir, always knew." His gaze unfocused for a moment, his voice weakened. "Your mama, bless her soul, she thought better of me. She made me want to try, made me want to be something, but you—" a rattle caught in his chest "—you knew she was too good for the likes of me. I could see it in your eyes."

Denial teetered on Nick's tongue before he swallowed it. "Mama deserved a better life than you gave her."

"She did, that's a fact." The old man closed his eyes with a sigh. To Nick's horror, a tear seeped out, slipped silently down into the brittle gray hair matted just above his ear. "When I lost your mama, I just couldn't go on. Nothing mattered no more, not living, not dying, not even raising my boy up right. So I drank because I wasn't no good for nothing else, and I drank so I wouldn't see the bruises on your body and the blame in your eyes—" he rattled a breath "—and I drank so I wouldn't remember that the only person who ever gave a fig about me was waiting for me on the other side, and I drank to hurry up the time when I could go to her, hear her sweet voice telling me that it didn't matter what folks said because she knew I was a good man."

Nick squeezed the bed rail until his knuckles ached. Breath came in shallow gasps, a series of small hissing sounds as air struggled into his lungs and fought its way back out again.

All the grief and the loneliness surrounding his mother's death resurfaced in a massive surge, wiping out the emotionless void. He remembered the tears, the ache so deep he hadn't believed it possible to survive. It had never occurred to him that his father was also suffering, that the man whose only visible emotion was drunken anger could possibly have experienced the same pain, the same exquisite loss. "You loved her, didn't you? You truly loved her."

Only when Lou opened his eyes did Nick realize he'd spoken aloud. "She was my whole life."

"You still had a life. You had a son."

"A son who wished his papa had died instead of his mama." The truth shook Nick to the marrow. Lou sighed, allowed his eyelids to slip shut. "I didn't blame you, boy. Always knew you was ashamed of me. Hell, I was ashamed of myself, but I couldn't stand seeing you look at me like I was some kind of freak. Couldn't stand it."

Nick didn't know what to say. Everything his father had said was true. Nick had been ashamed of him. As a child he'd had reason to be. As a man he understood the heartache, the insecurity, the crush of failure. And the loneliness of having no one to love.

Nick had survived because he'd found the one thing his father had lost, someone who believed in him, a compassionate juvenile court officer who'd taken an angry youngster under his wing and given him confidence to make a decent life for himself. For the first time since his mother's death, someone had shown faith in Nick.

It had been a turning point in his life.

Now he gazed into his father's hollow eyes and realized that but for the grace of God and a kind-hearted stranger, that could have been his own future. Lou Purcell had also lost the only person who'd loved him, who'd believed in him more than he'd believed in himself, who'd had faith in him as a human being and as a man, but no one had stepped into that void for his father. Not a friend, not a neighbor, not a stranger, not even his own son. Lou Purcell had been cut adrift by the world.

Squaring his shoulders, Nick took a shuddering breath. "It seems we have some lost years to make up for."

A thin smile stretched his parched lips, belying the sadness in his eyes. "Too late for that, Son."

"It's never too late."

"I let you down, boy, let you down bad. Wasn't a proper dad when you needed one. Can't go back now."

"No one can ever go back, but we can always go forward."

"You're a man fully growed. Don't need me now, and I sure as hell ain't gonna let myself need you. Got some pride left, yes sir, got me some pride."

"Then why did you ask the doctor to call me?"

Lou's gaze clouded. He glanced away. "Don't know for sure. To say goodbye, I guess, apologize for all the whippings you took. You didn't deserve what I done to you, boy, never deserved it. I wish things had been different."

"Things can be different if you want them to be. The doctor says if you stop drinking and take care of yourself you could have a lot of years ahead of you." Lou sighed, closed his eyes as if resigned to his fate. Nick wasn't about to let his father give up. "I know you don't think you're wanted or needed, Pop, but you're wrong. I need you." A lump wedged in Nick's throat as he nodded toward the open door of the room. "He needs you, too."

Baffled, Lou followed his son's gaze to the small, wide-eyed child hovering in the doorway. "Who's this?"

Nick motioned Bobby inside, slipped an arm around the youngster's shoulders. "This is your grandson."

"Grandson?" The old man's eyes widened, grew moist. "I got me a grandson?"

"Yes, Pop," Nick said quietly. "Looks like we both have a second chance."

In the hallway Chessa watched the interaction between Nick, his father and her own son. She couldn't hear what was being said, but when Bobby flung himself across the older man's bed, sobbing, she saw Lou Purcell lay a fragile hand on the boy's head and gaze up at his own son with wonder in his eyes.

Touched by the poignant reunion, she backed away from the door, seated herself on a smooth wooden bench across the hall.

A few minutes later Nick emerged. He sat beside her, stoic and expressionless. "He's asleep. Bobby wants to sit with him for a while. Is that all right with you?"

"Of course." She lifted his hand, cupped it between her palms. "Are you okay?"

"Yes."

Judging by his ashen complexion, she doubted that. "You were alone with your father for quite a while."

"We talked."

Silenced by instinct, she noted the turmoil in his gaze and waited.

"He knew," Nick said finally. "He knew I was

ashamed of him, knew I wished that it had been him who died instead of my mother.''

''Oh.'' She squeezed his hand. ''You were a child.''

He turned his haunted gaze on her. ''Can you imagine what that must have done to him, how he must have felt to know that his own son wished him dead?''

''You were a little boy heartbroken over the loss of your mother. I'm sure he understands that you didn't really mean it that way.''

''I did mean it that way. I could have been there for him, but I wasn't. I turned my back on my own father.''

''Tell me about it.''

He angled a glance. At first she thought he'd refuse. Instead, he slipped an arm around her shoulders, drawing her close as if he was the one consoling her. He spoke quietly, describing memories of the mother he'd adored for her gentle ways and loving spirit, and how her death had shattered him. Then Nick revealed the secret pain he'd shared with no one else in the world.

It was a secret that broke Chessa's heart.

That night, Chessa stared into the darkness of her own bedroom, remembering the pain in Nick's eyes, the stoic set of his jaw. He'd spoken quietly, as if describing a scene from a movie, the plot of a little-read book. There was no empathy for himself, no pity for the suffering child he'd once been. There was only resignation, a quiet sadness, the courage of a man so filled with compassion for others that there was none left for himself.

The words haunted her, words that had once splintered a young man's spirit, and crushed a broken soul. *You ain't no son of mine,* Nick's father had shouted. *Ain't my blood.*

Remembering those words and the silent torment in Nick's eyes as he'd revealed them, Chessa turned her face into her pillow and wept for the man who could not weep for himself.

Chapter Eight

"Ain't bad." Lou Purcell peered through the
doorway of the spacious room. A muscle below his
ear twitched. "For an old folks' home."

Nick sighed, set a suitcase packed with his father's
meager possessions inside the room. "This is the finest medical clinic and rehabilitation facility in the
state."

"A place for sick drunks." Lou shrugged. "Same
difference."

A week of rehashing the argument had grown tire-
some. "Would you prefer that rat-infested trailer
where you could drink yourself to death without in-
terference?"

"No, Grampa, no!" Bobby leaped forward, grasping the old man's hand. "Dad says you have to take
good care of yourself so you can come and live with
us after Mom and Dad—" The child's eyes snapped
open, as if he'd inadvertently revealed a deep, dark
secret. "I mean, we've got a really cool guest room

at our house, and Mom says it's okay if you stay there after you get all better.'' Biting his lip, Bobby angled a questioning look at Nick, who offered a wink and a reassuring nod. Their secret was still safe. Bobby expelled a massive breath, rolling his eyes as if to say, ''Boy, *that* was close!''

Without noticing the silent communication between his son and grandson, Lou focused on Chessa, who fidgeted with the strap of a stuffed duffle slung over her shoulder. ''That right, Chessie-gal?''

She glanced up with a smile, but it was Nick upon whom her gaze settled. ''You're welcome to stay with us as long as you wish, Lou. We'd love to have you.''

The older man cleared his throat, blinked rapidly, as if trying to dislodge the irksome moisture gathering in his eyes. ''That's right nice of you, real nice.''

A soothing warmth slipped along Nick's nape as Chessa gazed at him. Those beautiful eyes, lips so lush and sweet they haunted a man's dream and a melodic laugh that settled in his chest like liquid sunshine.

He was hooked, all right. Utterly, completely, totally enamored. Not only was Chessa Margolis the most beautiful, most wonderful woman on earth, she was also the kindest and most compassionate.

Nick didn't know what he would have done without her this past week. It was Chessa who'd located an alcohol rehabilitation program with a faculty of physicians to monitor his father's chronic medical condition. It was also Chessa who'd volunteered her own home for Lou's postrehabilitation care, much to Bobby's delight, since he and his newly found grampa had become closer in a single week than Nick had managed in a lifetime. Oddly enough, he didn't resent the closeness between his son and his father. He cherished it.

Family, real family. Nick knew how much family meant to Bobby. Until that moment he hadn't realized it meant just as much to him.

Puffing his cheeks, he eased his breath out slowly. When the emotional surge passed, he gently grasped his father's elbow, guiding the shuffling man to a pleasant armchair beside a sun-bright window. "Everything has been settled, Pop. All you have to do is follow doctor's orders and build up your strength. Looks to me like you've got a pretty snazzy place to do that."

No sooner had Lou lowered himself into the chair than Bobby scampered over, flushed with excitement. "Look, Grampa, you can see the duck pond."

Lou obliged the happy child by glancing out the window. "Always liked ducks." He paused a beat. "Good eating."

Bobby's double take would have been comical except for his horrified expression. "You can't eat ducks, Grampa!"

"Sure you can. Have to catch 'em first. They're tricky rascals." Before the child could protest, Lou angled a conspiratorial grin at Nick, who instantly recognized his own macabre love of tomfoolery mirrored in his father's twinkling eyes.

As a child he'd seen it, seen the teasing grin, watched the pranks his father pulled encouraged by his mother's appreciative laughter. Over the years, jocular memories had been overshadowed by the grief, the shame, the sadness. Images of happier times came back in a dizzying rush. Details flashed through his mind, images of birthday cakes and laughter, of crooked Christmas trees studded with homemade decorations, and of the whittled oak bow his father had carved for him as a gift.

There had been lazy days at a nearby fishing hole, when a sober Lou had tutored his young son's quest for striped bass. There had been idyllic afternoons in the woods stalking elk for the family's winter pantry. There had been joy in Nick's childhood. There had been love in his home. He'd just forgotten that for a while. Remembering centered him, gave him balance. He felt whole again.

"Grampa!" Bobby's high-pitched voice yanked Nick out of the past. "You don't really eat ducks, Grampa, you're just kidding me."

"You think so, do you?"

"Yep, unless you were winking at Dad because you think he's real cute."

The boy hunched his little shoulders, covered his mouth, and emitted an infectious giggle that spread around the room like a sweet scent. Chessa laughed, Nick laughed, and most amazing of all, Lou laughed. Not a thin chuckle or a wimpy tee-hee, either. No, sir, this was a throw-back-the-head, roar-from-the-gut, honest-to-goodness belly laugh the likes of which Nick hadn't heard since before his mother had died.

Bobby had released Lou's laughter, shattered the barrier of self-proclaimed misery as Nick never could. He was proud, so proud he felt as if his heart might just swell up and explode from his chest. This precious child was his blood, his legacy to the world. Nick couldn't take his eyes off the exuberant youngster who scampered around the room expounding the virtues of his grandfather's temporary quarters. "And a table and chairs, and a really big dresser—" the youngster bounded over to fling himself on the large bed "—and a neat television." He rolled over, eyes enormous. "Does Grampa have cable, Dad?"

Nick hoisted a suitcase to the foot of the bed, flipped it open to unpack it. "I don't know, Son."

"If he doesn't, can we buy him a satellite dish?"

"Sure, why not?"

"Cool." Beaming, Bobby scooted off the bed and returned to his grandfather's side.

Chessa crossed the room, set the duffel on the floor outside the bathroom door. "I'll do that," she murmured, taking the shirt Nick had just retrieved. "Why don't you and Bobby take Lou for a tour of the facility? By the time you get back, I'll have his things unpacked, and he'll feel more comfortable."

"Maybe later." When a covert glance confirmed that his son and his father were still gazing out the window, he watched Chessa lean forward to add another folded shirt to the stack beside the suitcase. Her hair slid forward, exposing her delicate nape. Drawn, Nick nipped lightly, then brushed a trail of moist kisses along the back of her neck.

She shivered, didn't seem to notice that the final shirt was upside down and sideways on the otherwise neat pile. "Stop," she whispered, and tilted her head to allow him better access.

He accepted the invitation with pleasure, tracing a moist line from the curve of her throat upward, then nibbling her earlobe until she purred like a sated cat.

"You taste good," he murmured. "Intoxicating, like sweet wine."

A sigh slipped out on a breath. "We are not alone, you know."

"I know." Snaking an arm around her waist, he pulled her close, feathered kisses from her jaw to her brow. "And that's a pity."

Pretending to ignore him, she sloppily slapped each carefully unpacked shirt back into the suitcase from whence they came. When she noticed what she'd done, her cheeks flamed with embarrassment. "This is your fault."

"I certainly hope so." Delighted, Nick chuckled, nudged her hair with the tip of his nose. "I enjoy distracting you." A nip, a taste, a soft murmur against her scented skin.

She shuddered, straightened, glanced past him to assure herself that she would not be overheard, then whispered with surprising conviction. "If you don't cut that out, my son, your father and this bed are liable to witness some rather surprising activity."

Instantly aroused by the sensual image, he splayed his hand at the small of her back, pressed her forward until her breasts flattened against his chest. "We won't always have an audience."

Clear blue eyes focused upward to his, smoldering with a desire that mirrored his own. "I'm counting on that."

His thumb brushed a stray wisp of hair from her cheek. "So am I," he said quietly. "So am I."

"Dad?" It took a moment to readjust his focus and turn toward the source of the high-pitched sound. "You're gonna come to my game tomorrow, aren't you?"

"Of course I am." Somehow he managed to sound relaxed enough to conceal the fact that a sensitive part of him threatened to burst from his slacks. "Wouldn't miss it."

Satisfied, Bobby returned his attention to his grandfather, and Nick furtively adjusted himself. "And after the game," he whispered, "you and I are going to spend a romantic evening. Alone."

"Are we?" An airy smile, a nonchalant shrug, neither of which concealed the anticipation in her eyes. "What do you have in mind?"

"If I told you—" he lifted her left hand, pointedly caressed her ring finger with the pad of his thumb "—it wouldn't be a surprise."

The day was blustery, with a sky streaked by wind-whipped clouds and the interstate crowded with speeding traffic. Nick checked his rearview mirror, punched the accelerator to veer into the fast lane, then merged into northbound Highway 505 on the outskirts of Vacaville. Traffic eased after the transition, would ease even more when he reached the Highway 5 interchange a few miles up the freeway.

He glanced at his dash clock, tightened his grip. It was past four. Bobby's game had already started. He knew his son would be disappointed by his tardiness, but would forgive him once he learned that tonight would be the culmination of the plans he and his son had secretly devised. A bag of special items lay on the seat beside him, items to implement the special event that his sly son had deftly orchestrated. Candles. Fresh raspberries. A spray of red roses. Everything he needed for a romantic evening, a night that would change all their lives forever.

A velvet lump pressed against his heart, protecting the precious symbol tucked in his breast pocket. The reminder chilled his palms, evoked a bead of icy moisture along his upper lip. This was the most important day of his life.

And he was very, very late.

Frustrated, he changed lanes again and increased his speed, cursing under his breath at the familiar ring of his cell phone, which was buried somewhere beneath the bag. He reached for it, alternately glancing at the road and the seat until he felt the smooth plastic cell phone beneath his hand.

As he flipped the on switch with his thumb, a familiar nasal whine set his teeth on edge. Nick's reply was less than gracious. "Whatever it is, Roger, it can wait."

"No it can't," Barlow insisted, sounding almost apoplectic. "I've taken the liberty of checking into Ms. Margolis's past, and found a—"

"You've done what?" Stunned, Nick stared at the phone as if attempting to visualize the pompous twit on the other end. In less than a heartbeat he returned his attention to the road, and grated angrily through clamped teeth, "On whose authority have you invaded Chessa's privacy in this manner? Certainly not mine. Her personal life is none of your business, Roger, and neither is mine. I thought I'd made that clear."

"I know, I know, and I'm sorry, but I've located a woman who went to school with Ms. Margolis and was apparently one of her best friends." A rush of air was followed by a sucking sound, as if Roger had emptied his lungs in a single breath, then refilled them all at once. "The woman's name is Jacqueline

Shane-MacAllister. I found her living in Connecticut with a husband and three kids.''

"I don't care if you found Jimmy Hoffa living in a subway tunnel with a gay gorilla and a staff of trained rats." Brake lights flashed from the line of traffic. He eased up on the gas. "It's none of your business, dammit. What part of that statement do you not understand?"

"This is important, Nick. Please, hear me out."

The nasal voice rose into a wail, words mingled with the screech of tires. A quarter mile up the highway, a semitrailer fishtailed wildly, belching smoke from locked wheels. The acrid smell of burning rubber reached Nick's nostrils at the same moment a small vehicle broadsided the skidding big rig.

Nick watched in horror, mesmerized by the chain reaction of carnage as the line of cars crashed, crunched and crushed into each other, one by one by one. A blinding flash, a scream of twisting metal. Nick dropped the phone, stomped the brake. The phone crashed against the dashboard. Romantic notions whipsawed through the air. Impact was imminent. Nick knew it, was braced for it, understood this could be his final moment on earth.

But all he could think about was what Roger had just told him.

At halftime Bobby raced to the bleachers, sweaty, grimy, eyes huge with hope. "Is Dad here yet?" His anxious gaze scanned the crowd, then the parking lot. "Did he see my goal?"

"No, sweetheart, I'm sorry." Chessa softened it with a smile. "He'll see it later. I'm sure Molly got it on tape."

Reflexively Bobby glanced toward the field where Danny's very pregnant mom juggled her two-year-old in one arm while focusing the palm-size video camera to record her own son gulping a sports drink behind the goal net. "It's not the same."

"I know." Biting her lip, Chessa gazed toward the parking lot, swallowed a surge of disappointment when a gray sedan glided close enough for her to see that it wasn't Nick's car. "He'll be here soon."

Bobby's face crumpled. "He promised, Mom, he promised."

"He'll be here." Pasting on a bright smile, she brushed a sweat-dampened curl of hair from his worried little face. "You'd better go, sweetie. Coach is calling you."

Heaving a sigh, Bobby glanced at the tall man in the purple Muddog jacket, then cast a final longing look at the parking lot before loping back across the field to join his teammates.

Nick still hadn't arrived when the second half began. He hadn't arrived when the Muddogs scored their second goal. He hadn't arrived when the clock ticked toward the final minutes of the game.

When the last whistle blew, the Marysville Muddogs had won their very first game. Bobby should have been happy and proud. He should have joined his teammates in celebrating a great victory. Instead, he walked away from a crowning moment in his young life with tears in his eyes because his father hadn't been there to share it.

"I know, Lou, but I thought he might have stopped by for a visit and lost track of time." Ducking under the long phone cord, Chessa peered out the kitchen window for the third time in as many minutes. Interrupting Lou's monologue about awful food in the complex cafeteria, Chessa blurted, "I'll call you tomorrow. Bobby's waiting for me to tuck him in."

She hung up, guilt at her brusqueness overshadowed by fear. A secret voice in her mind whispered that Nick would never have broken a promise to Bobby unless something terrible had happened.

Something terrible.

With a ragged gasp, she pushed the thought out of her mind, refused to allow herself to even consider the possibility. There was a logical explanation. There had to be.

Another glance at the dark street in front of the house, and she quickly dialed Nick's cellular phone. After two rings the line automatically switched over to drone, "The customer you're trying to reach is unavailable." Since she'd heard the same message twenty times over the past two hours, she hung up, weary to the bone.

"Mom?" Bobby's voice scratched through the intercom. "Is Dad here yet?"

Chessa rubbed her eyes, punched the open microphone button on the control panel. The red light flashed on. "No, sweetie, not yet. He'll be here soon."

Rustling sounds filtered through the speaker, as if Bobby had shifted beneath the covers. The intercom in his room was located beside the bed and remained in the open microphone position at all times so his somnambulistic cries could be heard throughout the house. He was in bed now, Chessa guessed, although he'd probably been looking out his window when he'd first called out to her.

More out of habit than expectation, Chessa went back to the kitchen window and stared into the blackness. No headlights yet. But he'd be here. He must have just gotten hung up at the office, that's all. Perhaps a meeting had lasted longer than he'd anticipated. Of course he rarely had meetings scheduled for Saturdays, but a man who owned a thriving business had to be flexible. He *could* have had a meeting. Perhaps he'd even tried to call her. Chessa had always despised answering machines, considering them irksome and impersonal. She made a mental note to purchase one first thing Monday morning.

"Mom?"

She answered without moving from her post in front of the window. "Yes, sweetie?"

"You'll tell me when Dad gets here, right?"

"Of course."

"I'm not gonna go to sleep until he comes."

"I know."

"But, umm, if I do, you know, accidentally—"

"I'll wake you up right away, sweetheart."

A pause, a rustle. "Okay."

The intercom fell silent. Chessa stood there, staring out into blackness, fighting the gnawing terror spreading deep inside her. She'd already called Nick's home phone, his work phone, his cell phone and the answering service he'd given her for emergencies. She'd left messages everywhere and had yet to find a real human with whom to speak.

She really did hate answering machines.

Something terrible had happened.

"No, everything is fine."

Something terrible.

"No!"

Bobby's frightened voice spun her around. "Who are you talking to, Mom? Is Dad here?"

Swallowing a lump of pure terror, she forced an even tone. "Not yet, sweetie. I promise I'll tell you the moment he arrives."

A heavy sigh. "Okay."

Frightened and frustrated, Chessa pivoted on the slick tile, strode past the blinking intercom into the living room as if she actually had a plan. She jerked to a stop when she realized she didn't, and stood there listening to the silence.

Mugsy unfurled from the sofa with a yawn. She actually heard the quiet swish of the cushion easing beneath the animal's soft weight. From across the room a clock ticked. She'd never noticed that before, had been unaware that the triangular timepiece made any sound at all. Suddenly the noise was unbearable, like the maddening beat of a frantic heart. She couldn't stand it.

Desperate to drown out the nerve-racking tick, she snatched the remote from the steamer-trunk coffee table, thumbed on the television and absently flipped from channel to channel in a futile attempt to distract herself.

She'd cycled the dial at least twice when something familiar caught her eye. A newscast, with film of a chain-reaction accident involving dozens of vehicles. It was awful, a mass of smoking, twisted wreckage, with rescue units tending the injured and other victims standing around, glazed and shaken by the carnage.

Something terrible had happened.

Three people had died. Dozens had been injured.

The film was graphic, the sight terrible, but it was a road sign in the distance that captured Chessa's attention. The accident had happened just a few miles south of the Marysville turnoff along a stretch of highway that Nick traversed a dozen times a week. He would have taken that same route today.

Something terrible.

Chessa began to shake uncontrollably. She knew. Dear God, she knew.

Chapter Nine

By nine that evening Chessa had retreated to her basement workshop where a halfhearted attempt to distract herself was a miserable failure. She'd mislabeled one order, sealed two others without enclosing a packing slip and was in the process of recounting the contents of yet another carton when she heard the thump of footsteps upstairs.

"Bobby?" A glance at the intercom console confirmed the blinking red light. The speaker was open, so she called out. "Bobby, sweetie, are you awake?" The monitor was silent. Another thump propelled her upstairs, where light sprayed from the kitchen, along with a peculiar rustling noise. "Bobby?"

Heart hammering, she rushed through the living room, steadied herself on the doorjamb. A gasp caught in her throat.

Rumpled and disheveled, seeming unconcerned that his expensive charcoal business suit was as wrinkled as a Shar pei's nose, Nick stood at the sink arranging a spray of crimson roses in a porcelain bud vase.

He glanced over his shoulder. "You forgot to set the alarm again. What would you do if I was some crazed, psychotic mistletoe thief?" With a frantic sob, she bolted across the room and flung herself into his waiting arms. Nick embraced her tenderly, stroking her hair. "If that's how you'd greet a crazed psychotic, you must be a holy terror with people you actually like."

Laughing and crying at the same time, Chessa gripped a fistful of wrinkled jacket with one hand, used the other to wipe away her tears. "I've been so worried."

That clearly surprised him. "About me?"

"Of course about you. You said you'd be here by four, then you weren't, and Bobby was so upset because you didn't see his goal, and you wouldn't answer your phone, and there was this horrible accident out on the interstate, and—" A shudder worked its way from her chin to her chest. "I thought something terrible had happened to you." Her gaze settled on a purplish lump just below his hairline. "My God, you're hurt."

"Hmm?" He absently touched his forehead before dismissing the injury with a shrug. "It's nothing." He pressed his palm against her cheek, eyes darkening to a smoldering glow. "Were you really worried?"

"Terrified." The memory brought a fresh surge of tears. He wiped them away with his thumb, regarding her with an expression of wonder. Chessa couldn't stop shaking. "I saw all those mangled cars, all those injured people on television—"

"Shh." He hugged her fiercely, pressing his cheek to her temple. "It's okay, honey, I'm okay."

"You wouldn't answer your phone." A muffled whine, like that of a frightened child. She hated the sound, hated the way she clung to him with such desperation, but was helpless to control her grasping fingers. Fractured by terror, her strength finally shattered, leaving her weak, boneless, on the verge of collapse. During those agonized hours when she'd feared she might have lost him, she'd realized just how much he meant to her.

She was in love with him. Deeply, profoundly, with every breath in her body, every fiber of her soul.

Stroking her cheek, Nick brushed his lips above her brow. His breath warmed her skin, soothed the frenetic rhythm of her heart. "The cell phone wasn't working. It was smashed...in the collision." She stiffened. He was ready for that, and held her firmly against him. "Yes, I was involved in the accident you saw on television."

All she could manage was a whisper. "What happened?"

"My car was clipped from behind, and spun into the median," he said. "From then on, it was pretty much chaos. Those of us who weren't injured helped those who were until the rescue units arrived, then we were interviewed and reinterviewed by more police officers than I've ever seen in one place. By the time I hitched a ride to the garage where my car had been towed, and arranged for a rental, it was so late I knew the game was long over, so I headed for the nearest fast-food place, and here I am."

"Yes," she whispered, feathering her fingertips

over his dear face to assure herself he was real. "Here you are."

"Mom!"

Chessa blinked while her fuzzy mind assimilated the familiar sound.

"Mom, Mom, where are you?"

Her son's panic spun her around. "I'm here, sweetie, I'm right here."

The monitor crackled with sleepy relief. "Okay." A rustle, a soft sigh, then silence.

"He's not really awake," she told Nick. "I promised I'd rouse him the moment you arrived."

She took a step before he stopped her. "Let me go to him," he said. He smiled, touched a fingertip to her lips. "When I get back, I'll put the finishing touches on dinner."

Suddenly Chessa was hungrier than she'd ever been in her life. "You've hunted and gathered. I'll beat it into submission and fling it on a plate."

He flinched. "I was hoping for something a bit more romantic."

"Romance is in the eye of the beholder." She kissed him square on the mouth, then whispered against his lips. "Hurry back?"

"Count on it." He studied her intently, a gaze both probing and clouded, posing a silent question while protecting the sanctity of his own thoughts. What he sought wasn't clear. When he blinked, the odd expression was gone. A moment later, so was he.

Baffled, Chessa listened to his footsteps fade on the stairs, then his voice crackled through the monitor. "Hey, buddy." A bed spring squeaked. "Sorry I missed your game."

The muffled reply was heavy with sleep. Nick spoke again, although his reply was inaudible.

A sense of supreme well-being washed over her. The man she loved, the child she adored, safe, secure and home. Home.

Comforted by the hum of voices from the intercom, she retrieved her best china from the cupboard and proceeded to set an elegant table more appropriate to a holiday feast than a humble meal of boxed chicken and plastic potato salad. She found candles in the bag Nick had brought, along with a bottle of sparkling faux champagne and a container of fresh raspberries so bright and luscious they made her mouth water.

Smiling foolishly, she glided about the familiar room as if floating on a pillow of air. A melody circled her mind, a song strummed in her heart. Life was glorious. She was madly, deeply, desperately in love.

The intercom squeaked again, as if a weight had lifted from Bobby's bed. "Did you ask her, Dad?"

The child's voice was slightly muffled, but the words were distinguishable, as was Nick's reply. "Not yet, Son."

"You're gonna, right?" More inaudible discussion. Chessa set a carefully arranged platter of chicken on the table, straining to hear. "Dad...? Don't turn off the hall light." Nick's reply was too distant to be discerned. "'Night, Dad. I love you." Bedclothes rustled once, and the intercom fell silent.

I love you.

Chessa's heart felt as if it had been squeezed. Love. Instinct told her this would be a night of love. And it was just the beginning.

* * *

Flickering candles bathed the darkened kitchen with a golden glow. Soft music floated from the living room stereo. A spray of roses adorned a table of fine china, crystal goblets and the remnants of their meal. Fresh raspberries garnished fluted stemware from which they'd sipped bubbling beverage and toasted a future that suddenly seemed brighter than diamonds. Nick had gazed into her eyes as if she were the most precious person on earth.

It had been the most beautiful evening of Chessa's life, and it was far from over.

Across the table Nick suddenly heaved a nervous sigh and touched his jacket, worrying what appeared to be axle grease smeared beside his limp lapel. A similar smudge adorned his white dress shirt, so stained and wrinkled by his earlier ordeal that it looked as if it had been yanked out of a laundry hamper and tossed on as an afterthought.

He cleared his throat, reached into his jacket to retrieve something and held it in his closed hand. "This evening hasn't gone exactly the way we'd planned." He paused to moisten his lips. "Bobby thought I should hide this beneath the raspberries in your champagne glass, but I was afraid you'd swallow it." A sheepish grin, an endearing shrug. "It's been that kind of a day."

Chessa sat there, stunned and silent.

Inhaling deeply, Nick squared his shoulders and studied her with that same probing gaze that had baffled her earlier in the evening. Before she could blink, he extended his hand and unfurled his fingers to reveal an indigo velvet box. She stared at it as if she'd never seen such a thing before.

"We've all become very close these past weeks,"
Nick was saying. "You and Bobby and me." He
coughed, shifted. "Er, the three of us. Like a family."

As Chessa stared at the elegant box nestled in his
palm, he suddenly snapped it open to reveal a cluster
of twinkling diamonds. It took a moment for her
numbed mind to realize the dazzling jewels were
mounted on a golden band. "Bobby thinks we should
get married."

Her head snapped up. "Bobby thinks?"

"I do, too, of course. I mean, given the amount of
time we spend together, how much we have in common, legalizing our relationship makes sense."

"You make it sound like a business merger."

"Oh." Crestfallen, he blinked nervously, set the
ring box on the table so he could rub his palms together. "I'm sorry. I've never done this before." He
took a massive breath, plucked the ring from its satin
pillow and lifted her hand. A quiver of emotion
quickened his speech. "I can't imagine what my future would be like if you and Bobby were not a part
of it. I want to spend the rest of my life with you,
Chessa...if you'll have me."

Her heart was trying to pound its way out of her
chest. "Are you really asking me to marry you,
Nick?"

"I suppose so." He paused a beat. "I mean, yes,
of course I am."

It was all Chessa had wanted, a dream come true.
And she was terrified. Marriage was too sacred to be
built on deception. But the truth could destroy them.

"Nick. I have to tell you—" The words caught in
her throat. He slipped the ring on her finger, regarded

it with odd dispassion, as if it had suddenly evolved from a symbol of eternal love to just another shiny bauble adorning a stranger's hand.

The weight of it felt peculiar to Chessa, cool rather than warm, and heavier than seemed natural. It seemed to compress around her finger as if in warning.

"By the way," Nick said softly. "Does the name Anthony Carlyle mean anything to you?"

The moment the question rolled off his tongue, Nick regretted it. Regretted it because every drop of color drained from Chessa's face. Regretted it because he hadn't planned to ask and because he feared the answer.

She swayed in her chair, steadied herself against the edge of the table. "Who told you about him?"

A fist of fear clamped inside his chest. "An associate who had no business prying into your life but chose to do so, anyway."

"I see."

The terror in her eyes affected him like a body blow. "Never mind. It doesn't matter."

"It matters." Eyes that only moments ago had sparkled with joy were now glazed, hollow. "You've done me the honor of asking me to be your wife. You have a right to know." Sensing his protest, she raised her palm like a shield. "No, please. Let me finish."

"All right." It wasn't all right, Nick knew that. The moment she confirmed what his heart already knew, nothing would ever be all right again.

Trembling, she clasped her hands together, studied the diamonds twinkling against her pale finger. "Anthony's father was the founder of Carlyle Electronics. You're familiar with the company, of course."

"Of course." Everyone in Weaverton was familiar with the town's largest employer.

"Anthony and I were high-school sweethearts." She spoke in a dull monotone, as if reciting dry facts out of an encyclopedia. "His parents didn't approve of our relationship, but we didn't care. We were young, foolish and very much in love."

Nick nodded as if his heart hadn't been ripped out. He didn't want to hear any more. "It was a long time ago. It doesn't affect us." He wanted only to silence her, to stop her from uttering the words that would change their lives forever.

A quiver of her lip was the only indication she'd heard him, and she would not stay silent. "When I discovered I was pregnant, I assumed Anthony would marry me. His father wouldn't hear of it. Eugene Carlyle was a powerful man, who'd use any means, even coercion, to get what he wanted. He threatened to disown Anthony, to ruin my father's career."

It all poured out then, all the pain, all the chaos, all the terror of a young girl abandoned by those she had trusted most. She described every detail of that long-ago night when her naïveté had been shattered and her innocence betrayed. As she spoke her eyes glazed, as if she'd returned to the stately parlor of the Carlyle mansion as a disinterested visitor. She dispassionately described the scene through the eyes of one who hadn't actually lived the grief. In part, Nick suspected, because she dared not open the floodgate of emotion by reliving the anguish of that terrible time.

"In the end Anthony's father turned him against

me, against the child we had created together." She shrugged without feeling. "A few months after Bobby was born, Anthony died in a traffic accident without having ever seen or acknowledged his son."

An icy calm settled in the pit of Nick's stomach. He wanted to hold her, to comfort her, but betrayal was an angry sword, and the hilt fit too well in his fist. "So that summer night on the bluff...?"

The question hung like candle smoke in an airless room.

Averting her gaze, Chessa slowly shook her head. "I wasn't with you, Nick. It wasn't me."

A sharpness ripped through him, as if he'd turned the sword upon himself. "In that case, I'm curious as to how I fit into all of this clandestine activity."

A single tear escaped to slide down her face. "I needed a name for the birth certificate."

Nick didn't have to ask why his name had been chosen. Son of the town drunk, a young man whose morals were genetically suspect, and who would most likely spend most of his life safely tucked in some faraway prison. "So Bobby's real father rots in a wormy grave, and the dumb schlep whose name you plucked out of a hat is gullible enough to show up on your doorstep. You can't seem to buy a break, can you?"

She shook her head, uttered a soft moan. "I tried to tell you Bobby wasn't your son."

"Yes, you did." The image flashed back, her stunned expression when he'd marched into her life, her angry denials and his arrogant persistence. He'd believed what he wanted to believe. "I guess you could say we both got what we deserved."

More angry with himself than with her, he pushed

away from the table, stood so quickly he nearly knocked the chair over.

Startled, Chessa straightened, extended a hand as he strode toward the door. "Nick, wait!" He paused, glanced over his shoulder and saw the panic in her eyes. Her lips moved soundlessly, as if testing the shape of words they could not form, then her shoulders slumped in resignation. They gazed at each other for the length of a heartbeat before she finally spoke. "I'm so sorry."

Pain and pride kept him from crumbling. "I know." Then he walked out of her life.

A part of her heart went with him.

Chessa didn't blame Nick for leaving. She blamed herself. She'd convinced herself that when a truth isn't believed, the lie no longer matters. She even convinced herself that given enough time, a lie could become the truth.

Whether the delusion had been madness or desperation no longer mattered. Bobby had needed a father. Nick had needed to be one. In the end Chessa had loved them both too much to destroy a relationship that had brought so much happiness into all of their lives.

Now she felt cold inside. Empty. Candlelight danced from her finger, refracted by the dazzling jewels that for a brief and shining moment had offered such hope, and such joy. It had been an illusion, of course. If she'd been honest with herself, she'd have acknowledged that a relationship formed on a foundation of deceit was doomed from the start.

But if Nick hadn't asked the question, hadn't spoken Anthony's name, she wondered if she would have ever had the courage to reveal the truth—the shattering truth that her beloved son would never, ever know the man who fathered him. Perhaps she would have perpetuated the lie, continued to deceive both the son she adored and the man with whom she had fallen so deeply in love.

Chessa didn't know. She would never know.

Moisture gathered in her eyes. Dancing lights on her finger blurred, the brilliant sparkle distorted by tears. She slid the ring from her finger, tucked it back into its satin cushion, and closed the velvet box. The ring didn't belong to her, had never belonged to her. Only the memories were hers to keep. The good memories and the bad, the joy and the sorrow.

She gathered those memories now, spread them out in her mind and relived them all, cherished them all. Darkness closed slowly, quietly. A candle dimmed, its flickering flame burned lower until it dipped into a pool of melted wax and was destroyed by that which had created it.

An exquisite ache spread deep in her chest, a throb of loss beyond any grief she'd experienced.

He was gone. She loved him, Bobby loved him, and he was gone.

Bolting upright, Chessa clutched her throat. *Bobby.* Dear God, what would she say to her son? How could she ever explain that the man he adored as a father, a mentor, a friend was gone forever because of her lies? How could she tell her son that death, which so terrified him, had irrevocably claimed the man who had given him life?

Frantic now, Chessa struggled to gather her wits, decide what to tell him, when to tell him, how to tell him. She blew out the final flickering candle, plunging the kitchen into complete darkness. As she turned toward the living room doorway, a blinking red light caught her eye. It was the intercom, signaling that the microphone function was engaged.

She stared stupidly at it, mentally digesting an implication too horrible to believe. The speaker was open. Erotic suggestions over potato salad and raspberry champagne, dreams of a future as a family, all had been broadcast directly to her son's room. Everything they'd said throughout the evening, every seductive word, every passionate murmur, every sob, every tear, every confession.

Every lie.

Air rushed from her lungs as if punched out. She spun through the doorway, sprinted up the stairs and into her son's room.

Light sprayed in from the hallway. Curtains flapped. A rush of cold air chilled her to the bone. The window was open. The bed was empty.

Bobby was gone.

It was well after midnight when Nick reached the reservoir bluff overlooking Weaverton. A few cars lingered in discreet shadows, as was usual on a Saturday night. Nick ignored them, parked on the edge of the cliff to gaze out at the view, just as he'd done a decade earlier.

Above him, stars twinkled against velveteen blackness, and moonlight edged the bank of indigo clouds settled over the Sierra. Below him, town lights sparkled like candlelight and diamonds.

Inside him, a heart splintered by pain, a loss so acute he felt as if a part of himself had been surgically removed. All that he'd believed, all that he'd trusted, everything he'd cared about, allowed himself to care about, had been built on a lie. It was a betrayal of the cruelest kind. He couldn't forgive it.

He wouldn't forgive it.

In the distance, a muffled engine roared to life. Headlights flashed. A car eased from the shadows, disappeared down the winding road. After a while the second vehicle left. Nick barely noticed. He was alone, alone with his pain, alone with his memories, those that were real, and those he'd created for himself.

Stars slipped across the heavens, constellations dipping below the horizon as others revealed themselves in the night sky.

Beyond the windshield, a specter appeared. A swish of sable hair, gleaming blue eyes, pink lips curved in a knowing smile. The face of his dreams. Chessa's face, outside the vehicle, outside of his life, yet enticing him to join her.

His mind had known, had always known. His heart simply wouldn't listen. For the first time, Nick understood why, why he'd created illusion as reality, why he'd pushed himself into Chessa's life despite her protests, why he'd drowned out the truth while clinging to the lie.

Nick had changed. He couldn't keep his emotions at bay anymore, couldn't pretend that financial success was the measure of a man. For the first time in his life, he finally understood what was truly important. And he was awed by the truth.

It was an hour before dawn now. A new day was beginning. For Nick, the rising sun symbolized release of darkness, a sunlight of the soul. Because in realizing that he'd always known the truth, he could

deal with his reasons for having ignored it. Simple
reasons, really. The moment he'd laid eyes on
Chessa, he'd fallen in love with her, a love that had
grown stronger and deeper by the day.

Accepting that Bobby wasn't his blood-child had
been difficult, and he'd been angry with Chessa for
having deceived him. Disappointment and anger
paled in comparison to the pain of envisioning a future without the two people he loved most in this
world. In every way that mattered, Chessa and Bobby
were the family he'd always longed for, providing
his life with a depth he hadn't realized was missing.

He realized it now. Everything was suddenly clear.
Bobby may not be the child of his body, but he was
the son of his soul. Chessa was the love of his life.
He belonged to them.

He belonged.

As the first spray of warmth touched the valley,
Nick drove the dusty road past the creek where
Bobby had gathered cattails, past ancient oaks still
heavy with mistletoe. Anxiety tightened his grip on
the steering wheel, joy tempered by instinctive apprehension. He was going home.

But even as he sped toward the home of his heart,
a voice in his mind whispered that he never should
have left.

Chapter Ten

By the time Nick pulled onto the familiar road just outside of Marysville, clouds had slipped down the mountainside to block dawn's promised warmth. A chill wind swooped through the valley swirling autumn leaves on patchy lawns. Nearly bare limbs vibrated as if frightened of the storm to come.

Nick saw the police cruisers, three of them, parked outside Chessa's house. Old habits die hard. Instinct took over, a gut-level fear of law enforcement from the bad old days when the sight of a squad car automatically triggered "fight or flight" syndrome. He hit the brake, broke out in a cold sweat, half expecting to see officers escort his drunken father to a squad car, a sight all too vivid in his memory.

Nick's own experience had been even more terrifying. He could still feel the cold shackles on his wrist, hear the crackle of a police scanner in the front of the cruiser. He remembered the quiet conversation of officers in the front seat chatting about duty rosters, plans for a weekend barbecue, everyday talk about everyday life, oblivious to the terrified teenager trembling in the back seat.

Every detail was fresh in his mind. He could still feel the pinch of metal biting his flesh, still smell the lingering terror of those who'd gone before him. All the memories roared back, knotting his gut, icing his skin.

Police cars. A lot of them. In front of Chessa's house.

It hit him like a sledgehammer. *Chessa's house.* Dear God, something was wrong, terribly wrong.

Panic boiled into his throat, nearly choking him, drowning painful memories in a flood of fresh fear. Punching the accelerator, he swerved behind a squad car, slammed to a stop, then sprinted toward the house where several uniformed officers shuffled like nervous watchdogs, and men in street clothes studied crushed flowers beneath the second-story windows.

As Nick headed toward the porch, a police officer moved forward to cut him off. "Are you a member of the family?"

"What's happened, what's wrong?" Without awaiting a reply, Nick stepped around him, would have bolted for the porch had the officer not grasped his arm.

"May I see some identification, please?"

"Identification?" Nick stared at him as if he'd never heard the word before, was vaguely aware of a heavyset, middle-aged woman who approached from the vicinity of the front porch.

"It's all right, officer. He's…a friend."

After the officer nodded and resumed sidewalk patrol, the woman studied Nick intently, with eyes so familiar and blue that he knew immediately who she was. He'd seen her before, a long time ago. She'd been thinner then, with long, lustrous hair the same glossy brown as her daughter's, hair that was now dulled with age, framing a face that was puffed by extra pounds and lined by passing years.

He acknowledged her with a nod. "Mrs. Margolis."

"Please, call me Marjorie." She offered a tense smile, regarded him with a strange combination of curiosity and apprehension. "You resemble your mother, you know. She was a lovely woman. I wish I'd taken the time to know her better."

The comment took him aback only momentarily. "Where's Chessa?"

A sadness clouded her eyes, a faraway melancholy that shook Nick to his toes. "She didn't want me to call, you know. She didn't think you'd come." Her smile loosened. "I knew you would."

"You called me?"

Marjorie tilted her head, as was her daughter's habit, and absently smoothed a brittle strand of graying hair wisping from a twisted bun at her crown. "You didn't get my message?"

Bewildered and more frightened than he'd ever been in his life, Nick shook his head without further explanation. "Is Chessa ill? Has she been hurt? I told her to keep the alarm set, I begged her to—"

"No, no, Chessa's fine." Marjorie blinked, chewed her lower lip. "It's Bobby," she said finally. "He's run away."

"Is that all?" For a moment, giddy relief rushed through him. Kids ran away all the time. Nick had done so himself more times than he could count.

Then his attention focused on the uniformed officers establishing a blue perimeter around the soccer-worn lawn, and realized that such a large presence was an abnormal response to a childish tantrum.

Marjorie Margolis seemed to read his mind. "Bobby has been gone for nearly nine hours, ever since he overheard the two of you talking last night and learned—" closing her eyes, she pressed pudgy clenched hands against an ample bosom "—that you weren't his father."

Nick's stomach twisted so quickly it nearly emptied itself. "My God." His skin went cold, vision blurred, and for a moment he feared he might be ill. The entire conversation flashed into his mind like a filmstrip at triple speed. He remembered it all, every crushing detail from the description of how the elder Carlyles had rejected their own grandchild, to the tragic death of Bobby's biological father and the deliberate deception that had followed. Bobby had heard it all, every shattering word.

After which Nick had simply waltzed away, leaving Chessa to deal with the aftermath.

"I have to talk with her," he murmured, and scoured his eyelids with his fingertips. He sucked in air, waited until the dizziness passed. "Please."

"She's inside, with the detectives." The woman grasped his arm as he started for the door. "It wasn't her fault, you know." Her hand fell away when he regarded her with confusion. "Her father and I put your name on the birth certificate. Chessa didn't know anything about it until after it was done. We're to blame, not her."

The terror in the woman's eyes stunned him. It was almost as if she believed the confession would lead to her own death. Although a portly woman, there was a fragility about her that touched him. He laid a gentle hand on her shoulder. "You did what you thought best to protect your daughter and grandchild. There was a time I wouldn't have understood that. I understand it now."

Grateful tears eased into her eyes. She grasped the hand on her shoulder, squeezed it. "Go. Chessa needs you."

The human mind is a wondrous thing. During times of severe stress, it props up the body, strengthens the soul. Chessa stood erect, supported by knees locked into position, and a paternal arm encircling her quivering shoulders.

"It is that man," James was saying. "Find him and you'll find my grandson."

The detective sighed, tucked a rumpled notepad in his jacket pocket. "We'll check out the boy's father, Mr. Margolis, just as we're checking out a report that a child matching your grandson's description was seen hitchhiking on the west-bound on-ramp of the interstate." He turned his attention toward Chessa. "Is there anything else you can tell us about this argument you believe the boy overheard, ma'am, anything at all?"

She raised her chin, willed herself not to cry. "Only that if Bobby is attempting to reach Nick, he's done so out of disappointment in me. None of this is Nick's fault. He's not to blame for my lies—" she cast a pointed stare at her father "—for our lies."

Wincing, James Margolis avoided his daughter's gaze. "Purcell is a convicted felon. He's involved in

my grandson's disappearance, and I insist you do
something about it."

"That's enough," Chessa said as she spun away,
saw her father's stunned expression as his arm
slipped from her shoulders and fell to his side.
"Don't you get it, Daddy? Bobby wasn't kidnapped,
he wasn't enticed to leave out of some perverse ven-
detta. My son ran away because he was hurt, because
he was heartbroken, because everyone he loved had
lied to him, and because he'd just learned that the
man he thought was his father—"

"Chessa, please." James angled an anxious glance
toward the detective who was listening with obvious
interest. "This is a private matter."

"Not anymore, Daddy, it's hurt too many people.
I'm through covering for you and Mom, I'm through
covering for myself. This is all my fault. I'm Bobby's
mother. He trusted me. Nick trusted me. Now they're
both gone."

"No, they're not."

The familiar voice enveloped her like a loving
touch. She turned, touched her throat.

He stood in the foyer like a rumpled god, even
more disheveled than he'd been the night before, and
even more beautiful. "Nick." The beloved name
rolled from her lips like a whisper. He opened his
arms, and she ran to him. "Bobby's gone," she
sobbed, allowing bottled emotions to surge forth un-
fettered. "He heard what we said last night, and he
ran away."

James stepped forward. "You don't know what he
heard, Chessa. This is not the time to discuss—"

She whirled like a she-cat defending its young.
"Stop it, Daddy, stop it right now! I know my son.

I know what he heard, I know what he felt, I know it here.'' She laid a hand against her chest, felt the frightened thud of her own heart pounding beneath her palm. ''The time for lies is over. All that matters now is finding my son.''

''Our son,'' Nick said quietly. He turned her in his arms, brushed a knuckle along her moist cheek. ''And we will find him.''

Before Chessa could respond, the detective stepped forward. ''Mr. Purcell, I have a few questions if you don't mind.''

Nick paled slightly, issued a curt nod. ''Of course.''

''When was the last time you saw your, er, son?''

''Last night about nine o'clock. Bobby was in bed. I went to say good-night to him.''

''Was there any indication that the boy was troubled or upset?''

''No, none.''

''Did he say anything that seemed out of the ordinary?''

''No.''

''Did he express anger with his mother or any other member of the family?''

''No, he was happy because—'' Nick's voice cracked slightly. He cleared his throat, spoke firmly. ''Because he knew I was going to ask Chessa to be my wife.''

Across the room James Margolis sucked an audible breath.

The detective merely raised a brow. ''And the boy was pleased by this?''

''Yes, very pleased. Bobby and I had been talking about it for days. It had been our secret—'' Nick paused a beat. "Secret," he murmured as if the word had suddenly taken on a new significance. "Our secret."

"Nick, what—?"

"I know where he is." Grasping Chessa's arm, Nick guided her out the front door, around the yard and toward the river.

She ran to keep up with him, vaguely aware that her parents, along with the detective and two uniformed officers, were following.

They headed to the levee road, rushed along the meandering river, with its treacherous undercurrents and deadly debris lurking beneath a deceptively calm surface. Instinctively she slowed, her heart racing in fear.

"He's not there," Nick said quietly. "Bobby is safe. Trust me."

There was no one on earth she trusted more. "I do."

He paused, gazed deep into her eyes for less than a heartbeat before guiding her down the levee bank toward a massive granite ledge. He hoisted himself up, reached down to assist Chessa, then led the way into a large weeping bush. Using her arms as a shield against the stinging twigs, she pushed through the opening into a small bush cave.

Bewildered, she glanced around, saw no evidence of her son. Nick swore softly. Panic resurfaced with a vengeance when she saw his perplexed frown. "Is this where he's supposed to be?" she asked. "Is it?" When he didn't answer, she clutched his arm in panic. "He's not here, Nick. You said you knew, you said—"

"Lots of secret places," Nick murmured, then appeared to startle himself, as if unaware he'd been speaking aloud. He slipped his arm from Chessa's panicked grasp, took her hand and led her out the other side.

They emerged in a forested cluster of conifer and oak studded with granite outcroppings and dozens of huge buck brush similar to the one through which they'd just passed. Shading his eyes, Nick gazed up into an oak to which a few brown leaves still clung. "Bobby?" There was no response, and the nearly barren limbs offered a clear view to the top. Bobby was not there.

The detective thrashed his way through the bush cave, followed by a muttering policeman. A moment later Chessa's parents emerged, white-faced and panting.

Marjorie wheezed, extended a pleading hand, which fell limply to her side when her husband embraced her. Grief circled their eyes, making them look older, more fragile. Blame and resentment drained away in an instant. For the first time in years, Chessa realized how much she loved them.

"Wait here," Nick said to no one in particular, then he headed toward a cluster of bushes edging a small clearing. One by one he peered into each clump, until he finally parted the thorny branches and disappeared into the mass of leaves.

That's when she heard it, a rumbling whisper, a sleepy reply, muffled voices issued from within the twisted foliage. Chessa took a hesitant step forward, not daring to believe that her mind wasn't playing tricks on her. Crisp leaves crunched beneath her shoe. A pebble tilted her off balance. She steadied herself on a drooping oak branch, then moved closer to the brushy clump of brush from which the voices emanated.

Leaves rustled, twigs scratched. Suddenly the bush parted as Nick backed out into the clearing, hunched over as if cradling something precious in his arms. He straightened, turned, tightened his grip on the groggy youngster clinging to his neck.

With a gasp of joy, Chessa leaped forward. "Bobby! Oh, Bobby!"

Rubbing his eyes with a small fist, the child blinked at her. "Mom?"

Laughing and crying at the same time, Chessa inspected every inch of her son, mentally logging every scratch, every bruise, every tiny abrasion. Her fingers traced his grimy little face, her palms smoothed back a mass of hair, gritty with dirt and full of bits of crushed foliage. "Are you all right, sweetheart? You're not hurt? I've been so worried, you scared us all to death." Only when the rush of frantic questions had completely emptied her lungs did she notice the crackle of a radio, as one of the officers notified Dispatch that Bobby had been located, and heard the soft sobbing of her mother in the background.

Awake now, Bobby's huge eyes focused on the group at the far edge of the clearing, a moment before his gaze bounced off his mom to settle on the face of the man who held him. Tears spurted, sheeted down his face in dirt-stained waves. "You're not my real dad," he cried. "My real dad didn't want me."

Nick met Chessa's gaze for only a moment, long enough to read permission in her eyes. He settled cross-legged on the ground, gathering the heartbroken child in his lap. "You're right, I'm not your biological father, but I don't believe that your real father didn't want you."

"He didn't," Bobby insisted between sobs. "Mom said."

Kneeling beside them, Chessa held her son's hand. "I'm so sorry I didn't talk to you about this a long time ago. I should have, but I was afraid you'd be angry with me." The child blinked silently, forcing her to continue without reassurance. "When I told your—" she swallowed "—real father that we were going to have a child, his face lit up like it was Christmas, and he hugged me so tight I couldn't breathe. He was so happy, so thrilled. He did want you, sweetheart, he wanted you so much."

"But he went away."

"I don't believe he wanted to go away, Bobby. Your father and I were very, very young when we were blessed with you. We were both very happy, but we were kind of scared, too. Having a baby is such a big responsibility."

Bobby sniffed, wiped his nose with the back of his hand. "Did my real gramma and grampa make him go away?"

"To an extent, yes, I think they did, but only because he was their son and they loved him just as much as I love you. They were afraid he wasn't grown-up enough to be a father, and that made him worry that maybe they were right. I think he just needed time to sort things out for himself."

"He never came back." Bobby sniffed, angled a glance upward. "Nick came back."

The reminder squeezed at her heart. "Yes," she whispered. "Nick came back."

Sensing her voice had failed, Nick took over. "I

suspect your real dad would have come back too, son, if he could have. You understand that there was an accident, don't you?" When Bobby's lip quivered, Nick soothed him with a hug. "It wasn't your father's fault that he died. You know that, don't you?"

For a moment Chessa feared Bobby would burst into hysterics. His eyes darted, his breathing became rapid and shallow, his lips twisted into a bereaved knot.

He swallowed a sob, stared straight into Nick's eyes. "Jerry Morrison says his dad watches him from heaven," he said, referring to the playmate whose father had died years ago. "Do you think my dad is watching me?"

"Yes, Son, I do."

"That's not the same as having a real dad."

"No, it's not the same." Nick took a breath, swallowed hard. "I can't take the place of your real father. No one can. But I can try to be a dad to you, Bobby, and I promise to do the very best that I can. In my heart you will always be my son. I love you very, very much." His gaze swung to Chessa. "Just as I love your mother."

Chessa's heart skipped a beat, then thudded wildly. It was true. His eyes told her it was true. He did love her, he actually loved her. "I love you, too, Nick, with all my heart."

Bobby regarded them both. "So, like, if you guys love each other and stuff, how come we can't be a real family?"

Nick's slow smile made her dizzy. "I'd like nothing better, Son, but it's up to your mother."

Bobby's head swung around. "So, Mom, are you gonna marry Dad or what?"

A snicker slipped out before she could stop it. "Yes, I think maybe I will."

"Cool!" The boy beamed, turned back to Nick. "So are you gonna give her the ring?"

"Your Mom already has it."

"She does?" His grin faded as he studied her bare ring finger. "Aw geez, Mom, you didn't really swallow it, did you?"

Laughing, she reached out and hugged them both. "No, I didn't. The moment we get home we'll celebrate with a big ring ceremony, and we'll all plan the wedding."

"All of us? Gramma and both grampas, too?"

A glance over her shoulder revealed that her mother was smiling through her tears, as was her father, whose approving nod touched her almost as deeply as did his reddened eyes. "Yes, sweetheart, gramma and both grampas, too."

Slinging one small arm around Nick's neck, Bobby reached out to also embrace his mother. "We're gonna be a real family, aren't we?"

"We already are," Nick whispered. "We already are."

Epilogue

"Look, Sherrie, there's Grampa Lou." Shifting his
sister in the crook of his arm, Bobby pumped her
baby hand in a wave. Across the yard Grampa Lou
shifted in the lawn chair. His face cracked into a big
old grin, just like it always did when he saw Sherrie.
Grampa Lou said she was just about the prettiest
child God ever put on this here earth. Bobby figured
he was right.

Sherrie squeaked and drooled, happily whacked
her fat, bare tummy and bounced on her brother's
arm so hard he was afraid he'd drop her. She was
only eight months old. Bobby was crazy about her.
"Guess what I heard!" The baby swung around, focused her huge bright eyes as if dying of curiosity.
Bobby glanced around to make sure the gabbing
group of friends and relatives gathered for the Fourth
of July celebration didn't overhear his secret. "The
doctor says Grampa Lou's new liver is doing real
good," he whispered. "As long as he takes his med-

icine and doesn't start drinking again, he can pretty much do anything he wants, even get a job! And this is the really good part…'' Sherrie gleefully clapped her fat hands. ''He's gonna go to work for Dad.''

The baby gasped on cue, stuffed a fist into her soggy mouth.

''Yep, I heard him and Dad talking last night. Grampa Lou is gonna learn how to install security systems. He's real excited. Said it's gonna be real cool to be the boss's daddy. Said he expects special treatment.''

Duly impressed, the baby reached out to pinch Bobby's cheek, a habit that was painful enough to make her brother flinch, but endearing enough for him to allow.

At twelve, Bobby wasn't a kid anymore. He was in junior high now, as tall as Mom with feet bigger than Dad's. The way Bobby figured it, he was already grown-up. Had himself a girlfriend and everything, had given her a swell bracelet for Valentine's Day, so they were officially going steady. Mom thought that was kind of cute, but Dad had sat him down for a birds-and-bees talk that had embarrassed him half to death. Still, he thought it kind of cool, having a dad that cared enough to tell him stuff, even if it was stuff he already knew.

''Our dad is the best dad in the whole world,'' he told his sister, who grunted affably, poked a baby finger in her belly button, which was exposed by a short summer top embroidered with pink turtles. ''Look, Dad is wearing that stupid barbecue apron Mom bought him. He looks like a dork.''

That got Sherrie's attention. Her little head shifted, dark curls bouncing as she peered across a yard crammed with happy people, some balancing paper plates heaped with beans and potato salad, some gathered in chattering clumps, some just hanging out like Grampa Lou, waiting for the fireworks display Mom and Dad were planning for later that evening.

Mom was over by the wading pool with Gramma and Grampa Margolis. Every once in a while she'd slip a glance at the pot-bellied smoker where Dad was grilling chicken and steak. He really liked to barbecue. Right after he and Mom got married, Dad dragged home that fat smoker and had fired it up almost every weekend for the past two years. When it was raining, he'd move the cars out and barbecue in the garage, only he had to leave the door open to let the smoke out, so sometimes the rain would blow in and he'd get kinda wet.

He didn't mind, though. Heck, he didn't mind much of anything. Dad liked all the stuff that most kids' fathers gripe about, like mowing lawns and painting fences and coaching soccer, and he even liked grocery shopping, which was kinda cool on account of Mom was real busy with her business now. The basement got so crammed nobody could even walk down there, so Mom rented part of an old industrial building by the railroad tracks last year, and now she said that she needed an even bigger place because catalog orders had tripled in the past six months.

Bobby loved how happy his mom got when she talked about the business. She loved how happy his dad looked whenever Mom was happy, and she was happy pretty much all the time now. So was Robert James Margolis Purcell, which was Bobby's official

name ever since the adoption had been finalized. He
was real proud of that name.

Wafting smoke carried a tantalizing scent across
the yard. "Hmm, smells good," Bobby murmured,
sniffing toward the source of the delicious aroma.
"Too bad you can't eat steak and stuff, Sherrie.
You'd really like it."

The baby babbled as if expressing disappointment.

Hugging his sister close, Bobby maneuvered
through the milling throng to emerge a few feet from
his aproned father, who glanced over his shoulder
with a proud grin. "There you are." Dropping a
greasy spatula on a nearby table, Nick bent to kiss
Sherrie's damp forehead while slipping an arm
around Bobby's shoulders for a manly hug. "Getting
hungry, Son?"

"Sort of." He eyed the sizzling steaks until his
mouth watered. A sweet fragrance wafted in, a moment before his mother came up and ruffled his hair.
She nuzzled his neck, laughing when he pulled away.
"Aw, Mom, you keep treating me like a kid."

"I'm sorry, sweetheart." She wasn't sorry at all,
but that was okay, because Bobby kind of liked being
hugged and kissed all the time. He only grumbled
about it because that's what his buddies did. Mom
fussed with Sherrie's curly hair, smoothed her wrinkled little turtle top. "I'll take the baby for a while,
sweetheart, so you can go play with your friends."

Casting an indifferent glance toward the mowed
field where Danny and the group were engaged in an
impromptu game of stickball, Bobby protectively
shifted his sister away from his mother's outreached
hands. "Nah, that's okay. Sherrie and I are gonna go

hang out with Grampa Lou for a while. He's got a lot of neat stories she hasn't heard yet.''

His mom brushed her fingertips along Bobby's cheek. Her eyes were all dewy. ''You've been carrying her around all day.''

He shrugged. ''That's okay. She's not heavy.''

Mom sniffed like she was gonna cry or something, then hugged him all sloppylike. Bobby made a production of frowning, in case one of his friends happened to see the mushy display. She ruffled his hair again, gave him a teasing grin. ''You're the best big brother any little girl could have.''

The praise pleased him, but he just shrugged. ''If you guys would hurry up and have a boy, I could teach him how to play soccer and stuff.''

Mom giggled, got all jittery. When her face turned pink, Dad wiped his hand on his apron and slipped an arm around her waist. ''So a baby sister isn't enough, now you want a baby brother, too?'' He heaved a big sigh, looked at Mom the way Mugsy looks at a Thanksgiving turkey. ''Well then, we'll just have to see what we can do to accommodate that, won't we?'' He whispered something in Mom's ear that made her turn purple.

She swatted his chest. ''Nick! Stop that.''

''Never.'' He pulled her real close and kissed her right on the mouth.

Pretending not to notice, Bobby turned away, headed toward Grampa Lou. ''They do that all the time,'' he told his sister. ''They're always kissing and hugging and stuff. You'll get used to it.''

At that moment Bobby felt like the luckiest kid alive. He had a cool baby sister, the best mom in the whole world, and he had two real dads, one who

watched him from heaven, and one who took care of
him here on earth.

"You wanna know how you got here, Sherrie?"
The baby blinked up in fascination. "Well, it all
started with this nice old lady who makes really good
cookies and smells like flowers..."

The cat purred. The rocker creaked. Stroking the
contented animal curled in her lap, Clementine Allister St. Ives scanned another file. Intriguing, she
thought. A lonely widow, an angry, abandoned dad,
a pair of precious twins torn between the grandparents who raised them and the father they barely
know.

Closing the file, she leaned back in her rocker and
smiled. Santa Barbara was beautiful this time of year.
Deirdre would love it.

*   *   *   *   *

Sometimes families are made in the most unexpected ways!

Don't miss this heartwarming new series from
Silhouette Special Edition®, Silhouette Romance®
and popular author

DIANA WHITNEY

Every time matchmaking lawyer
Clementine Allister St. Ives brings a couple
together, it's for the children...
and sure to bring romance!

August 1999
I NOW PRONOUNCE YOU MOM & DAD
Silhouette Special Edition #1261
Ex-lovers Powell Greer and Lydia Farnsworth knew *nothing*
about babies, but Clementine said they needed to learn—fast!

September 1999
A DAD OF HIS OWN
Silhouette Romance #1392
When Clementine helped little Bobby find his father, Nick Purcell
appeared on the doorstep. Trouble was, Nick wasn't Bobby's dad!

October 1999
THE FATHERHOOD FACTOR
Silhouette Special Edition #1276
Deirdre O'Connor's temporary assignment from Clementine
involved her handsome new neighbor, Ethan Devlin—and
adorable twin toddlers!

Available at your favorite retail outlet.

Look us up on-line at: http://www.romance.net   SSEFTC

Looking For More Romance?

Visit Romance.net

Look us up on-line at: http://www.romance.net

Check in daily for these and other exciting features:

Hot off the press

View all current titles, and purchase them on-line.

What do the stars have in store for you?

Horoscope

Hot deals

Exclusive offers available only at Romance.net

Plus, don't miss our interactive quizzes, contests and bonus gifts.

PWEB

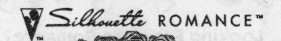

Silhouette ROMANCE™

VIRGIN BRIDES

**Your favorite authors
tell more heartwarming
stories of lovely brides
who discover love...
for the first time....**

July 1999 GLASS SLIPPER BRIDE
Arlene James (SR #1379)
Bodyguard Jack Keller had to protect innocent
Jillian Waltham—day and night. But when his assignment
became a matter of temporary marriage, would Jack's hardened
heart need protection...from Jillian, his glass slipper bride?

September 1999 MARRIED TO THE SHEIK
Carol Grace (SR #1391)
Assistant Emily Claybourne secretly loved her boss, and now Sheik
Ben Ali had finally asked her to marry him! But Ben was only
interested in a temporary union...until Emily started showing him
the joys of marriage—and love....

November 1999 THE PRINCESS AND THE COWBOY
Martha Shields (SR #1403)
When runaway Princess Josephene Francoeur needed a
short-term husband, cowboy Buck Buchanan was the perfect
choice. But to wed him, Josephene had to tell a *few* white lies,
which worked...until "Josie Freeheart" realized she wanted
to love her rugged cowboy groom forever!

Available at your favorite retail outlet.

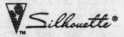

Silhouette®

Look us up on-line at: http://www.romance.net   SRVB992